THE SUSPECT

"We're looking for a stranger, six foot tall, wearing newish Dunlop Wellington boots size 10½, leather gloves and an old blue overcoat stained with blood. A man who travels on foot, who was in the area of North Fields between 11:10 and 11:45 on the night of the murder, who left in the direction of Okeford, taking with him one and a half feet of coaxial cable, a string of green beads and an imitation diamond clip. We're looking for a maniac, a man who kills for pleasure or the price of a meal . . . who can fly fifty feet through the air."

A MURDER OF QUALITY

Bantam Books by John le Carré
Ask your bookseller for the books you have missed

CALL FOR THE DEAD
THE HONOURABLE SCHOOLBOY
THE LITTLE DRUMMER GIRL
THE LOOKING GLASS WAR
A MURDER OF QUALITY
THE NAIVE AND SENTIMENTAL LOVER
A PERFECT SPY
A SMALL TOWN IN GERMANY
SMILEY'S PEOPLE
THE SPY WHO CAME IN FROM THE COLD
TINKER, TAILOR, SOLDIER, SPY

A MURDER
OF
QUALITY

John le Carré

BANTAM BOOKS

NEW YORK · TORONTO · LONDON · SYDNEY · AUCKLAND

823.9
L456m
1980

*This edition contains the complete text
of the original hardcover edition.*
NOT ONE WORD HAS BEEN OMITTED.

A MURDER OF QUALITY

*A Bantam Book / published by arrangement with
the author*

PRINTING HISTORY

*Walker & Company edition published August 1968
Bantam edition / January 1980
11 printings through July 1990*

ISBN 0-553-26443-5

*Bantam Books are published by Bantam Books, a division of Bantam
Doubleday Dell Publishing Group, Inc. Its trademark, consisting of the
words "Bantam Books" and the portrayal of a rooster, is Registered in U.S.
Patent and Trademark Office and in other countries. Marca Registrada.
Bantam Books, 666 Fifth Avenue, New York, New York 10103.*

PRINTED IN THE UNITED STATES OF AMERICA

RAD   20   19   18   17   16   15   14   13   12   11

A MURDER
OF
QUALITY

I

Black Candles

The greatness of Carne School has been ascribed by common consent to Edward VI, whose educational zeal is ascribed by history to the Duke of Somerset. But Carne prefers the respectability of the monarch to the questionable politics of his adviser, drawing strength from the conviction that Great Schools, like Tudor Kings, were ordained in Heaven.

And indeed its greatness is little short of miraculous. Founded by obscure monks, endowed by a sickly boy king, and dragged from oblivion by a Victorian bully, Carne had straightened its collar, scrubbed its rustic hands and face and presented itself shining to the courts of the twentieth century. And in the twinkling of an eye, the Dorset bumpkin was London's darling: Dick Whittington had arrived. Carne had parchments in Latin, seals in wax and Lammas Land behind the Abbey. Carne had property, cloisters and woodworm, a whipping block and a line in the Doomsday Book—then what more did it need to instruct the sons of the rich?

And they came; each Half they came (for terms are not elegant things), so that throughout a whole afternoon the trains would unload sad groups of black-coated boys on to the station platform. They came in great cars that shone with mournful purity. They came

1

to bury poor King Edward, trundling handcarts over the
cobbled streets or carrying tuck boxes like little coffins.
Some wore gowns, and when they walked they looked
like crows, or black angels come for the burying. Some
followed singly like undertakers' mutes, and you could
hear the clip of their boots as they went. They were
always in mourning at Carne; the small boys because
they must stay and the big boys because they must
leave, the masters because mourning was respectable
and the wives because respectability was underpaid; and
now, as the Lent Half (as the Easter term was called)
drew to its end, the cloud of gloom was as firmly settled
as ever over the grey towers of Carne.

Gloom and the cold. The cold was crisp and sharp
as flint. It cut the faces of the boys as they moved
slowly from the deserted playing fields after the school
match. It pierced their black topcoats and turned their
stiff, pointed collars into icy rings round their necks.
Frozen, they plodded from the field to the long walled
road which led to the main tuck shop and the town, the
line gradually dwindling into groups, and the groups
into pairs. Two boys who looked even colder than the
rest crossed the road and made their way along a narrow path which led towards a distant but less populated
tuck shop.

"I think I shall die if ever I have to watch one of
those beastly rugger games again. The noise is fantas-
tic," said one. He was tall with fair hair, and his name
was Caley.

"People only shout because the dons are watching
from the pavilion," the other rejoined; "that's why each
house has to stand together. So that the house dons can
swank about how loud their houses shout."

"What about Rode?" asked Caley. "Why does he
stand with us and make us shout, then? He's not a
house don, just a bloody usher."

"He's sucking up to house dons all the time. You
can see him in the quad between lessons buzzing round
the big men. All the junior masters do." Caley's com-

panion was a cynical red-haired boy called Perkins, Captain of Fielding's house.

"I've been to tea with Rode," said Caley.

"Rode's hell. He wears brown boots. What was tea like?"

"Bleak. Funny how tea gives them away. Mrs. Rode's quite decent, though—homely in a plebby sort of way: doilies and china birds. Food's good: Women's Institute, but good."

"Rode's doing Corps next Half. That'll put the lid on it. He's so *keen,* bouncing about all the time. You can tell he's not a gentleman. You know where he went to school?"

"No."

"Branxome Grammar. Fielding told my Mama, when she came over from Singapore last Half."

"God. Where's Branxome?"

"On the coast. Near Bournemouth. I haven't been to tea with anyone except Fielding." Perkins added after a slight pause, "You get roast chestnuts and crumpets. You're never allowed to thank him, you know. He says emotionalism is only for the lower classes. That's typical of Fielding. He's not like a don at all. I think boys bore him. The whole house goes to tea with him once a half, he has us in turn, four at a time, and that's about the only time he talks to most men."

They walked on in silence for a while until Perkins said:

"Fielding's giving another dinner party tonight."

"He's pushing the boat out these days," Caley replied, with disapproval. "Suppose the food in your house is worse than ever?"

"It's his last Half before he retires. He's entertaining every don and all the wives separately by the end of the Half. Black candles every evening. For mourning. Hells extravagant."

"Yes. I suppose it's a sort of gesture."

"My Pater says he's a queer."

They crossed the road and disappeared into the tuck shop, where they continued to discuss the weighty affairs of Mr. Terence Fielding, until Perkins drew their meeting reluctantly to a close. Being a poor hand at science, he was unfortunately obliged to take extra tuition in the subject.

The dinner party to which Perkins had alluded that afternoon was now drawing to a close. Mr. Terence Fielding, senior housemaster of Carne, gave himself some more port and pushed the decanter wearily to his left. It was his port, the best he had. There was enough of the best to last the Half—and after that, be damned. He felt a little tired after watching the match, and a little drunk, and a little bored with Shane Hecht and her husband. Shane was so hideous. Massive and enveloping, like a faded Valkyrie. All that black hair. He should have asked someone else. The Snows for instance, but he was too clever. Or Felix D'Arcy, but D'Arcy interrupted. Ah well, a little later he would annoy Charles Hecht, and Hecht would get in a pet and leave early.

Hecht was fidgeting, wanting to light his pipe, but Fielding damn well wouldn't have it. Hecht could have a cigar if he wanted to smoke. But his pipe could stay in his dinner-jacket pocket, where it belonged, or didn't belong, and his athletic profile could remain unadorned.

"Cigar, Hecht?"

"No thanks, Fielding. I say, do you mind if I . . ."

"I can recommend the cigars. Young Havelake sent them from Havana. His father's ambassador there, you know."

"Yes, dear," said Shane tolerantly; "Vivian Havelake was in Charles' troop when Charles was commandant of the Cadets."

"Good boy, Havelake," Hecht observed, and pressed his lips together to show he was a strict judge.

"It's amusing how things have changed." Shane Hecht said this rapidly with a rather wooden smile, as if it weren't really amusing. "Such a grey world we live in, now.

"I remember before the war when Charles inspected the Corps on a white horse. We don't do that kind of thing now, do we? I've got nothing against Mr. Iredale as commandant, nothing at all. What *was* his regiment, Terence, do you know? I'm sure he does it very nicely, whatever they do now in the Corps—he gets on so well with the boys, doesn't he? His wife's such a nice person. . . . I wonder why they can never keep their servants. I hear Mr. Rode will be helping out with the Corps next Half."

"Poor little Rode," said Fielding slowly; "running about like a puppy, trying to earn his biscuits. He tries so hard; have you seen him cheering at school matches? He'd never seen a game of rugger before he came here, you know. They don't play rugger at grammar schools—it's all soccer. Do you remember when he first came, Charles? It was fascinating. He lay very low at first, drinking us in: the games, the vocabulary, the manners. Then, one day it was as if he had been given the power of speech, and he spoke in our language. It was amazing, like plastic surgery. It was Felix D'Arcy's work of course—I've never seen anything quite like it before."

"Dear Mrs. Rode," said Shane Hecht in that voice of abstract vagueness which she reserved for her most venomous pronouncements: "So sweet . . . and such simple taste, don't you think? I mean, whoever would have dreamed of putting those china ducks on the wall? Big ones at the front and little ones at the back. Charming, don't you think? Like one of those teashops. I wonder where she bought them. I must ask her. I'm told her father lives near Bournemouth. It must be so lonely for him, don't you think? Such a vulgar place; no one to talk to."

Fielding sat back and surveyed his own table. The silver was good. The best in Carne, he had heard it said, and he was inclined to agree. This Half he had nothing but black candles. It was the sort of thing people remembered when you'd gone: "Dear old Terence—marvellous host. He dined every member of the staff during his last Half, you know, wives too. Black candles, rather touching. It broke his heart giving up his house." But he must annoy Charles Hecht. Shane would like that. Shane would egg him on because she hated

Charles, because within her great ugly body she was as
cunning as a snake.

Fielding looked at Hecht and then at Hecht's wife,
and she smiled back at him, the slow rotten smile of a
whore. For a moment Fielding thought of Hecht pastur-
ing in that thick body: it was a scene redolent of Lau-
trec . . . yes, that was it! Charles pompous and top-
hatted, seated stiffly upon the plush coverlet; she
massive, pendulous and bored. The image pleased him:
so perverse to consign that fool Hecht from the Spartan
cleanliness of Carne to the brothels of nineteenth-
century Paris. . . .

Fielding began talking, pontificating rather, with
an air of friendly objectivity which he knew Hecht
would resent.

"When I look back on my thirty years at Carne, I
realise I have achieved rather less than a roadsweeper."
They were watching him now—"I used to regard a
roadsweeper as a person inferior to myself. Now, I
rather doubt it. Something is dirty, he makes it clean,
and the state of the world is advanced. But I—what
have *I* done. Entrenched a ruling class which is distinguished by neither talent, culture nor wit; kept alive for
one more generation the distinctions of a dead age."

Charles Hecht, who had never perfected the art of
not listening to Fielding, grew red and fussed at the
other end of the table.

"Don't we teach them, Fielding? What about our
successes, our scholarships?"

"I have never taught a boy in my life, Charles.
Usually the boy wasn't clever enough; occasionally, I
wasn't. In most boys, you see, perception dies with pu-
berty. In a few it persists, though where we find it we
take good care at Carne to kill it. If it survives our efforts the boy wins a scholarship. . . . Bear with me,
Shane; it's my last Half."

"Last Half or not, you're talking through your hat,
Fielding," said Hecht, angrily.

"That is traditional at Carne. These successes, as
you call them, are the failures, the rare boys who have
not learned the lessons of Carne. They have ignored the

cult of mediocrity. We can do nothing for them. But for the rest, for the puzzled little clerics and the blind little soldiers, for them the truth of Carne is written on the wall, and they hate us."

Hecht laughed rather heavily.

"Why do so many come back, then, if they hate us so much? Why do they remember us and come and see us?"

"Because we, dear Charles, are the writing on the wall! The one lesson of Carne they never forget. They come back to read *us*, don't you see? It was from us they learnt the secret of life: that we grow old without growing wise. They realised that nothing happened when we grew up: no blinding light on the road to Damascus, no sudden feeling of maturity." Fielding put his head back and gazed at the clumsy Victorian moulding on the ceiling, and the halo of dirt round the light rose.

"We just got a little older. We made the same jokes, thought the same thoughts, wanted the same things. Year in, year out, Hecht, we were the same people, not wiser, not better; we haven't had an original thought between us for the last fifty years of our lives. They saw what a trick it all was, Carne and us; our academic dress, our schoolroom jokes, our wise little offerings of guidance. And that's why they come back year after year of their puzzled, barren lives to gaze fascinated at you and me, Hecht, like children at a grave, searching for the secret of life and death. Oh, yes, they have learned *that* from us."

Hecht looked at Fielding in silence for a moment.

"Decanter, Hecht?" said Fielding, in a slightly conciliatory way, but Hecht's eyes were still upon him.

"If that's a joke . . ." he began, and his wife observed with satisfaction that he was very angry indeed.

"I wish I knew, Charles," Fielding replied with apparent earnestness. "I really wish I knew. I used to think it was clever to confuse comedy with tragedy. Now I wish I could distinguish them." He rather liked that.

They had coffee in the drawing-room, where Fielding resorted to gossip, but Hecht was not to be drawn. Fielding rather wished he had let him light his pipe. Then he recalled his vision of the Hechts in Paris, and it restored him. He had been rather good this evening. There were moments when he convinced himself.

While Shane fetched her coat, the two men stood together in the hall, but neither spoke. Shane returned, an ermine stole, yellow with age, draped over her great white shoulders. She inclined her head to the right, smiled and held out her hand to Fielding, the fingers down.

"Terence, darling," she said, as Fielding kissed her fat knuckles; "so kind. And in your last Half. You must dine with us before you go. So sad. So few of us left." She smiled again, half closing her eyes to indicate emotional disturbance, then followed her husband into the street. It was still bitterly cold and snow was in the air.

Fielding closed and carefully bolted the door behind them—perhaps a fraction earlier than courtesy required—and returned to the dining room. Hecht's port glass was still about half full. Fielding picked it up and carefully poured the contents back into the decanter. He hoped Hecht wasn't too upset; he hated people to dislike him. He snuffed the black candles and damped their wicks between his forefinger and thumb. Switching on the light, he took from the sideboard a sixpenny notebook, and opened it. It contained his list of dining guests for the remainder of the Half. With his fountain pen he placed a neat tick against the name Hecht. They were done. On Wednesday he would have the Rodes. The husband was quite good value, but she, of course, was hell. . . . It was not always the way with married couples. The wives as a rule were so much more sympathetic.

He opened the sideboard and took from it a bottle of brandy and a tumbler. Holding them both in the same hand, he shuffled wearily back to the drawing room, resting his other hand on the wall as he went. God! He felt old, suddenly; that thin line of pain across the chest, that heaviness in the legs and feet. Such an effort being with people—on stage all the time. He hated to be alone, but people bored him. Being alone was like being tired, but unable to sleep. Some German poet had said that; he'd quoted it once, "You may sleep but I must dance." Something like that.

"That's how I am," thought Fielding. "That's how Carne is, too; an old satyr dancing to the music." The music grew faster and their bodies older, but they must dance on—there were young men waiting in the wings. It had been funny once dancing the old dances in a new world. He poured himself some more brandy. He'd be pleased to leave in a way, even though he'd have to go on teaching somewhere else.

But it had its beauty, Carne. . . . The Abbey Close in spring . . . the flamingo figures of boys waiting for the ritual of worship . . . the ebb and flow of children, like the seasons of the year, and the old men dying among them. He wished he could paint; he would paint the pageant of Carne in the fallow browns of autumn. . . . What a shame, thought Fielding, that a mind so perceptive of beauty had no talent for creation.

He looked at his watch. Quarter to twelve. Nearly time to go out . . . to dance, and not to sleep.

II

The Thursday Feeling

It was Thursday evening and the *Christian Voice* had just been put to bed. This was scarcely an historic event in Fleet Street. The pimply boy from Despatch who took away the ragged pile of page-proofs showed no more ceremony than was strictly demanded by the eventual prospect of his Christmas bonus. And even in this respect he had learned that the secular journals of Unipress were more provident of material charity than the *Christian Voice*; charity being in strict relationship to circulation.

Miss Brimley, the journal's editor, adjusted the air cushion beneath her and lit a cigarette. Her secretary and sub-editor—the appointment carried both responsibilities—yawned, dropped the aspirin bottle into her handbag, combed out her ginger hair and bade Miss Brimley good night, leaving behind her as usual the smell of strongly scented powder and an empty paper-tissue box. Miss Brimley listened contentedly to the clipping echo of her footsteps as it faded down the corridor. It pleased her to be alone at last, tasting the anti-climax. She never failed to wonder at herself, how every Thursday morning brought the same slight uneasiness as she entered the vast Unipress building and stood a little absurdly on one escalator after the other, like a drab parcel on a luxury liner. Heaven knows, she had run the

Voice for fourteen years, and there were those who said its layout was the best thing Unipress did. Yet the Thursday feeling never left her, the wakeful anxiety that one day, perhaps today, they wouldn't be ready when the despatch boy came. She often wondered what would happen then. She had heard of failures elsewhere in that vast combine, of features disapproved and staff rebuked. It was a mystery to her why they kept the *Voice* at all, with its expensive room on the seventh floor and a circulation which, if Miss Brimley knew anything, hardly paid for the paper-clips.

The *Voice* had been founded at the turn of the century by old Lord Landsbury, together with a Nonconformist daily newspaper and the *Temperance Gazette*. But the *Gazette* and the daily were long since dead, and Landsbury's son had woken one morning not long ago to find his whole business and every man and woman of it, every stick of furniture, ink, paper-clips and galley-pins, bought by the hidden gold of Unipress.

That was three years ago and every day she had waited for her dismissal. But it never came; no directive, no question, no word. And so, being a sensible woman, she continued exactly as before and ceased to wonder.

And she was glad. It was easy to sneer at the *Voice*. Every week it offered humbly and without fanfares evidence of the Lord's intervention in the world's affairs, retold in simple and somewhat unscientific terms the early history of the Jews, and provided over a fictitious signature motherly advice to whomever should write and ask for it. The *Voice* scarcely concerned itself with the fifty-odd millions of the population who had never heard of it. It was a family affair, and rather than abuse those who were not members, it did its best for those who were. For them it was kind, optimistic, and informative. If a million children were dying of the plague in India, you may be sure that the weekly editorial described the miraculous escape from fire of a Methodist family in Kent. The *Voice* did not advise you how to disguise the encroaching wrinkles round your eyes, or control your spreading figure; did not dis-

may you, if you were old, by its own eternal youth. It
was itself middle-aged and middle class, counselled caution to girls and charity to all. Nonconformity is the
most conservative of habits and families which took the
Voice in 1903 continued to take it in 1960.

Miss Brimley was not quite the image of her journal. The fortunes of war and the caprice of Intelligence
work had thrown her into partnership with the younger
Lord Landsbury, and for the six years of war they had
worked together efficiently and inconspicuously in an
unnamed building in Knightsbridge. The fortunes of
peace rendered both unemployed, but Landsbury had
the good sense, as well as the generosity, to offer Miss
Brimley a job. The *Voice* had ceased publication during the war, and no one seemed anxious to renew it. At
first Miss Brimley had felt a little ashamed at reviving
and editing a journal which in no way expressed her
own vague deism, but quite soon, as the touching letters
came in and the circulation recovered, she developed an
affection for her job—and for her readers—which
outweighed her earlier misgivings. The *Voice* was her
life, and its readers her preoccupation. She struggled to
answer their odd, troubled questions, sought advice of
others where she could not provide it herself, and in
time, under a handful of pseudonyms, became if not
their philosopher, their guide, friend and universal aunt.

Miss Brimley put out her cigarette, absently tidied
the pins, paper-clips, scissors and paste into the top
righthand drawer of her desk, and gathered together the
afternoon mail from her in-tray which, because it was
Thursday, she had left untouched. There were several
letters addressed to Barbara Fellowship, under which
name the *Voice* had, since its foundation, answered
both privately and through its published columns the
many problems of its correspondents. They could wait
until tomorrow. She rather enjoyed the "problem post,"
but Friday morning was when she read it. She opened
the little filing cabinet at her elbow and dropped the
letters into a box file at the front of the compartment.
As she did so, one of them fell on its back and she noticed with surprise that the sealed flap was embossed

with an elegant blue dolphin. She picked the envelope
out of the cabinet and looked at it curiously, turning it
over several times. It was of pale grey paper, very
faintly lined. Expensive—perhaps hand-made. Beneath
the dolphin was a tiny scroll on which she could just
discern the legend, *Regem defendere diem videre*. The
postmark was Carne, Dorset. That must be the school
crest. But why was Carne familiar to her? Miss Brimley
was proud of her memory, which was excellent, and she
was vexed when it failed her. As a last resort she
opened the envelope with her faded ivory paper knife
and read the letter.

> *Dear Miss Fellowship,*
>
> *I don't know if you are a real person but it
> doesn't matter, because you always give such
> good, kind answers. It was me who wrote last
> June about the pastry mix. I am not mad and I
> know my husband is trying to kill me. Could I
> please come and see you as soon as it's conve-
> nient? I'm sure you'll believe me, and understand
> that I am normal. Could it be as soon as possible
> please, I am so afraid of the long nights. I don't
> know who else to turn to. I could try Mr. Cardew
> at the Tabernacle but he wouldn't believe me and
> Dad's too sensible. I might as well be dead. There's
> something not quite right about him. At night
> sometimes when he thinks I'm asleep he just lies
> watching the darkness. I know it's wrong to think
> such wicked things and have fear in our hearts,
> but I can't help it.*
>
> *I hope you don't get many letters like this.*
>
> > *Yours faithfully,*
> > *Stella Rode (Mrs.)*
> > *née Glaston.*

She sat quite still at her desk for a moment, looking at the address in handsome blue engraving at the
top of the page: "North Fields, Carne School, Dorset."
In that moment of shock and astonishment one phrase
forced itself upon her mind. "The value of intelligence
depends on its breeding." That was John Landsbury's

favourite dictum. Until you know the pedigree of the information you cannot evaluate a report. Yes, that was what he used to say: "We are not democratic. We close the door on intelligence without parentage." And she used to reply: "Yes, John, but even the best families had to begin somewhere."

But Stella Rode *had* parentage. It all came back to her now. She was the Glaston girl. The girl whose marriage was reported in the editorial, the girl who won the summer competition; Samuel Glaston's daughter from Branxome. She had a card in Miss Brimley's index.

Abruptly she stood up, the letter still in her hand, and walked to the uncurtained window. Just in front of her was a contemporary window-box of woven white metal. It was odd, she reflected, how she could never get anything to grow in that window-box. She looked down into the street, a slight, sensible figure leaning forward a little and framed by the incandescent fog outside; fog made yellow from the stolen light of London's streets. She could just distinguish the street lamps far below, pale and sullen. She suddenly felt the need for fresh air, and on an impulse quite alien to her usual calm, she opened the window wide. The quick cold and the angry surge of noise burst in on her, and the insidious fog followed. The sound of traffic was constant, so that for a moment she thought it was the turning of some great machine. Then above its steady growl she heard the newsboys. Their cries were like the cries of gulls against a gathering storm. She could see them now, sentinels among the hastening shadows.

It might be true. That had always been the difficulty. Right through the war it was the same restless search. It might be true. It was no use relating reports to probability when there was no quantum of knowledge from which to start. She remembered the first intelligence from France on flying bombs, wild talk of concrete runways in the depths of a forest. You had to resist the dramatic, you had to hold out against it. Yet it might be true. Tomorrow, the day after, those newsboys down there might be shouting it, and Stella Rode *née* Glaston might be dead. And if that was so, if there was the remotest chance that this man was plotting to kill this woman, then she, Ailsa Brimley, must do what she could to prevent it. Besides, Stella Glaston had a claim on her assistance if anyone did: both her father and her grandfather had taken the *Voice*, and when Stella married five years ago Miss Brimley had put a couple of lines about it in the editorial. The Glastons sent her a Christmas card every year. They were one of the original families to subscribe. . . .

It was cold at the window, but she remained there, still fascinated by the half hidden shadows joining and parting beneath her, and the useless street lights burning painfully among them. She began to imagine him as one of those shadows, pressing and jostling, his murderer's eyes turned to sockets of dark. And suddenly she was frightened and needed help.

But not the police, not yet. If Stella Rode had wanted that she would have gone herself. Why hadn't she? For love? For fear of looking a fool? Because instinct was not evidence? They wanted fact. But the fact of murder was death. Must they wait for that?

Who would help? She thought at once of Landsbury, but he was farming in Rhodesia. Who else had been with them in the war? Fielding and Jebedee were dead, Steed Asprey vanished. Smiley—where was he? George Smiley, the cleverest and perhaps the oddest of them all. Of course, Miss Brimley remembered now. He made that improbable marriage and went back to research at Oxford. But he hadn't stayed there. . . . The marriage had broken up. . . . What *had* he done after that?

She returned to her desk and picked up the S-Z directory. Ten minutes later she was sitting in a taxi, heading for Sloane Square. In her neatly gloved hand she held a cardboard folder containing Stella Rode's card from the index and the correspondence which had passed between them at the time of the Summer Competition. She was nearly at Piccadilly when she remembered she'd left the office window open. It didn't seem to matter much.

"With other people it's Persian cats or golf. With me it's the *Voice* and my readers. I'm a ridiculous spinster, I know, but there it is. I won't go to the police until I've tried *something*, George."

"And you thought you'd try me?"

"Yes."

She was sitting in the study of George Smiley's house in Bywater Street; the only light came from the complicated lamp on his desk, a black spider of a thing shining brightly on to the manuscript notes which covered the desk.

"So you've left the Service?" she said.

"Yes, yes, I have." He nodded his round head vigorously, as if reassuring himself that a distasteful experience was really over, and mixed Miss Brimley a whisky and soda. "I had another spell there after . . . Oxford. It's all very different in peacetime, you know," he continued.

Miss Brimley nodded.

"I can imagine it. More time to be bitchy." Smiley said nothing, just lit a cigarette and sat down opposite her.

"And the people have changed. Fielding, Steed, Jebedee. All gone." She said this in a matter-of-fact way as she took from her large sensible handbag Stella Rode's letter. "This is the letter, George."

When he had read it, he held it briefly towards the lamp, his round face caught by the light in a moment of almost comic earnestness. Watching him, Miss Brimley wondered what impression he made on those who did not know him well. She used to think of him as the most forgettable man she had ever met; short and plump, with heavy spectacles and thinning hair, he was at first sight the very prototype of an unsuccessful middle-aged bachelor in a sedentary occupation. His natural diffidence in most practical matters was reflected in his clothes, which were costly and unsuitable, for he was clay in the hands of his tailor, who robbed him.

He had put down the letter on the small marquetry table beside him, and was looking at her owlishly.

"This other letter she sent you, Brim. Where is it?"

She handed him the folder. He opened it and after a moment read aloud Stella Rode's other letter:

Dear Miss Fellowship,
I would like to submit the following suggestion for your "Kitchen Hints" competition.
Make your basic batch of cake mixture once a month. Cream equal quantities of fat and sugar and add one egg for every six ounces of the mixture. For puddings and cakes, add flour to the required quantity of basic mixture.
This will keep well for a month.
I enclose stamped addressed envelope.

Yours sincerely,
Stella Rode (née Glaston).

PS.—Incidentally, you can prevent wire wool from rusting by keeping it in a jar of soapy water. Are we allowed two suggestions? If so, please can this be my second?

"She won the competition," Miss Brimley observed, "but that's not the point. This is what I want to tell you, George. She's a Glaston, and the Glastons have been reading the *Voice* since it started. Stella's grandfather was old Rufus Glaston, a Lancashire pottery king; he and John Landsbury's father built chapels and tabernacles in practically every village in the Midlands. When Rufus died the *Voice* put out a memorial edition and old Landsbury himself wrote the obituary. Samuel Glaston took on his father's business, but had to move south because of his health. He ended up near Bournemouth, a widower with one daughter, Stella. She's the last of all that family. The whole lot are as down to earth as you could wish, Stella included, I should think. I don't think any of them is likely to be suffering from delusions of persecution."

Smiley was looking at her in astonishment.

"My dear Brim, I can't possibly take that in. How on earth do you know all this?"

Miss Brimley smiled apologetically.

"The Glastons are easy—they're almost part of the

magazine. They send us Christmas cards, and boxes of chocolates on the anniversary of our foundation. We've got about five hundred families who form what I call our Establishment. They were in on the *Voice* from the start and they've kept up ever since. They write to us, George; if they're worried they write and say so; if they're getting married, moving house, retiring from work, if they're ill, depressed, or angry, they write. Not often, Heaven knows; but enough."

"How do you remember it all?"

"I don't. I keep a card index. I always write back, you see . . . only . . ."

"Yes?"

Miss Brimley looked at him earnestly.

"This is the first time anyone has written because she's frightened."

"What do you want me to do?"

"I've only had one bright idea so far. I seem to remember Adrian Fielding had a brother who taught at Carne. . . ."

"He's a housemaster there, if he hasn't retired."

"No, he retires this Half—it was in *The Times* some weeks ago, in that little bit on the Court page where Carne always announces itself. It said: 'Carne School reassembles today for the Lent Half. Mr. T. R. Fielding will retire at the end of the Half, having completed his statutory fifteen years as a housemaster.'"

Smiley laughed.

"Really, Brim, your memory is absurd!"

"It was the mention of Fielding . . . Anyway, I thought you could ring him up. You must know him."

"Yes, yes. I know him. At least, I met him once at Magdalen High Table. But——" Smiley coloured a little.

"But what, George?"

"Well he's not quite the man his brother was, you know."

"How could he be?" Miss Brimley rejoined a little sharply. "But he can tell you something about Stella Rode. And her husband."

"I don't think I could do that on the telephone. I

think I'd rather go and see him. But what's to stop you ringing up Stella Rode?"

"Well, I can't tonight, can I? Her husband will be in. I thought I'd put a letter in the post to her tonight telling her she can come to see me any time. But," she continued, making a slight, impatient movement with her foot, "I want to do something *now*, George."

Smiley nodded and went to the telephone. He rang directory enquiries and asked for Terence Fielding's number. After a long delay he was told to ring Carne School central exchange, who would connect him with whomever he required. Miss Brimley, watching him, wished she knew a little more about George Smiley, how much of that diffidence was assumed, how vulnerable he was.

"The best," Adrian had said. "The strongest and the best."

But so many men learnt strength during the war, learnt terrible things, and put aside their knowledge with a shudder when it ended.

The number was ringing now. She heard the dialling tone and for a moment was filled with apprehension. For the first time she was afraid of making a fool of herself, afraid of becoming involved in unlikely explanations with angular, suspicious people.

"Mr. Terence Fielding, please. . . ." A pause.

"Fielding, good evening. My name is George Smiley; I knew your brother well in the war. We have in fact met. . . . Yes, yes, quite right—Magdalen, was it not, the summer before last? Look, I wonder if I might come and see you on a personal matter . . . it's a little difficult to discuss on the telephone. A friend of mine has received a rather disturbing letter from the wife of a Carne master . . . Well, I—Rode, Stella Rode; her husband . . ."

He suddenly stiffened, and Miss Brimley, her eyes fixed upon him, saw with alarm how his chubby face broke into an expression of pain and disgust. She no longer heard what he was saying. She could only watch the dreadful transformation of his face, the whitening knuckles of his hand clutching the receiver. He was looking at her now, saying something . . . it was too late. Stella Rode was dead. She had been murdered late on Wednesday night. They'd actually been dining with Fielding the night it happened.

III

The Night Of The Murder

The seven-five from Waterloo to Yeovil is not a popular train, though it provides an excellent breakfast. Smiley had no difficulty in finding a first-class compartment to himself. It was a bitterly cold day, dark and the sky heavy with snow. He sat huddled in a voluminous travelling coat of Continental origin, holding in his gloved hands a bundle of the day's papers. Because he was a precise man and did not care to be hurried, he had arrived thirty minutes before the train was due to depart. Still tired after the stresses of the previous night, when he had sat up talking with Ailsa Brimley until Heaven knew what hour, he was disinclined to read. Looking out of the window on to an almost empty station, he caught sight, to his great surprise, of Miss Brimley herself making her way along the platform, peering in at the windows, a carrier bag in her hand. He lowered the window and called to her.

"My dear Brim, what are you doing here at this dreadful hour? You should be in bed."

She sat down opposite him and began unpacking her bag and handing him its contents: thermos, sandwiches and chocolate.

"I didn't know whether there was a breakfast car," she explained; "and besides, I wanted to come and see you off. You're such a dear, George, and I wish I could

21

come with you, but Unipress would go mad if I did. The only time they notice you is when you're not there."

"Have you seen the papers?" he asked.

"Just briefly, on the way here. They seem to think it wasn't him, but some madman. . . ."

"I know, Brim. That's what Fielding said, wasn't it?" There was a moment's awkward silence.

"George, am I being an awful ass, letting you go off like this? I was so sure last night, but now I wonder . . ."

"After you left I rang Ben Sparrow of Special Branch. You remember him, don't you? He was with us in the war. I told him the whole story."

"George! At three in the morning?"

"Yes. He's ringing the Divisional Superintendent at Carne. He'll tell him about the letter, and that I'm coming down. Ben had an idea that a man named Rigby would be handling the case. Rigby and Ben were at police college together." He looked at her kindly for a moment. "Besides, I'm a man of leisure, Brim. I shall enjoy the change."

"Bless you, George," said Miss Brimley, woman enough to believe him. She got up to go, and Smiley said to her:

"Brim, if you should need any more help or anything, and can't get hold of me, there's a man called Mendel who lives in Mitcham, a retired police inspector. He's in the book. If you get hold of him and mention me, he'll do what he can for you. I've booked a room at the Sawley Arms."

Alone again, Smiley surveyed uneasily the assortment of food and drink which Miss Brimley had provided. He had promised himself the luxury of breakfast in the restaurant car. He would keep the sandwiches and coffee for later, that would be the best thing; for lunch, perhaps. And he would breakfast properly.

In the restaurant car Smiley read first the less sensational reports on the death of Stella Rode. It appeared that on Wednesday evening Mr. and Mrs. Rode had been guests at dinner of Mr. Terence Fielding, the senior housemaster at Carne and brother of the late Adrian

Fielding, the celebrated French scholar who had vanished during the war while specially employed by the War Office. They had left Mr. Fielding's house together at about ten to eleven and walked the half mile from the centre of Carne to their house, which stood alone at the edge of the famous Carne playing fields. As they reached their house Mr. Rode remembered that he had left at Mr. Fielding's house some examination papers which urgently required correction that night. (At this point Smiley remembered that he had failed to pack his dinner jacket, and that Fielding would almost certainly ask him to dine.) Rode determined to walk back to Fielding's house and collect the papers, therefore, starting back at about five past eleven. It appears that Mrs. Rode made herself a cup of tea and sat down in the drawing-room to await his return.

Adjoining the back of the house is a conservatory, the inner door of which leads to the drawing room. It was there that Rode eventually found his wife when he returned. There were signs of a struggle, and certain inexpensive articles of jewelry were missing from the body. The confusion in the conservatory was terrible. Fortunately there had been a fresh fall of snow on Wednesday afternoon, and detectives from Dorchester were examining the footprints and other traces early on Thursday morning. Mr. Rode had been treated for shock at Dorchester Central Hospital. The police wished to interview a woman from the adjacent village of Pylle who was locally known as "Mad Janie" on account of her eccentric and solitary habits. Mrs. Rode, who was well known in Carne for her energetic work on behalf of the International Refugee Year, had apparently shown a charitable interest in her welfare, and she had vanished without trace since the night of the murder. The police were currently of the opinion that the murderer had caught sight of Mrs. Rode through the drawing-room window (she had not drawn the curtains) and that Mrs. Rode had admitted the murderer at the front door in the belief that it was her husband returning from Mr. Fielding's house. The Home Office pathologist had been asked to conduct a post-mortem examination.

The other reports were not so restrained: "Murder most foul has desecrated the hallowed playing fields of Carne" one article began, and another, "Science teacher discovers murdered wife in blood-spattered conservatory." A third screamed, "Mad woman sought in Carne murder." With an expression of distaste, Smiley screwed up all the newspapers except the *Guardian* and *The Times* and tossed them onto the luggage rack.

He changed at Yeovil for a local line to Sturminster, Okeford and Carne. It was something after eleven o'clock when he finally arrived at Carne station.

He telephoned the hotel from the station and sent his luggage ahead by taxi. The Sawley Arms was only full at Commemoration and on St. Andrew's Day. Most of the year it was empty; sitting like a prim Victorian lady, its slate roof in the mauve of half mourning, on ill tended lawns midway between the station and Carne Abbey.

Snow still lay on the ground, but the day was fine and dry, and Smiley decided to walk into the town and arrange to meet the police officer conducting the investigation of the murder. He left the station, with its foretaste of Victorian austerity, and walked along the avenue of bare trees which led towards the great Abbey tower, flat and black against the colourless winter sky. He crossed the Abbey Close, a serene and beautiful square of mediaeval houses, the roofs snow-covered, the white lawns shaded with pin strokes of grass. As he passed the west door of the Abbey, the soft snow creaking where he trod, the clock high above him struck the half-hour, and two knights on horseback rode out from their little castle over the door, and slowly raised their lances to each other in salute. Then, as if it were all part of the same clockwork mechanism, other doors all round the Close opened too, releasing swarms of black-coated boys who stampeded across the snow towards the Abbey. One boy passed so close that his gown brushed against Smiley's sleeve. Smiley called to him as he ran past:

"What's going on?"

"Sext," shouted the boy in reply, and was gone.

He passed the main entrance to the school and came at once upon the municipal part of the town, a lugubrious nineteenth-century fairyland in local stone, stitched together by a complexity of Gothic chimneys and crenel windows. Here was the town hall, and beside it, with the flag of St. George floating at its masthead, the Carne Constabulary Headquarters, built ninety years ago to withstand the onslaughts of archery and battering rams.

He gave his name to the Duty Sergeant, and asked to see the officer investigating the death of Mrs. Rode. The Sergeant, an elderly, inscrutable man, addressed himself to the telephone with a certain formality, as if he were about to perform a difficult conjuring trick. To Smiley's surprise, he was told that Inspector Rigby would be pleased to see him at once, and a police cadet was summoned to show him the way. He was led at a spanking pace up the wide staircase in the centre of the hall, and in a matter of moments found himself before the Inspector.

He was a very short man, and very broad. He could have been a Celt from the tin-mines of Cornwall or the collieries of Wales. His dark grey hair was cut very close; it came to a point in the centre of his brow like a devil's cap. His hands were large and powerful, he had the trunk and stance of a wrestler, but he spoke slowly, with a Dorset burr to his soft voice. Smiley quickly noticed that he had one quality rare among small men: the quality of openness. Though his eyes were dark and bright and the movements of his body swift, he imparted a feeling of honesty and straight dealing.

"Ben Sparrow rang me this morning, sir. I'm very pleased you've come. I believe you've got a letter for me."

Rigby looked at Smiley thoughtfully over his desk, and decided that he liked what he saw. He had got

around in the war and had heard a little, just a very
little, of the work of George Smiley's service. If Ben
said Smiley was all right, that was good enough for
him—or almost. But Ben had said more than that.

"Looks like a frog, dresses like a bookie, and has a
brain I'd give my eyes for. Had a very nasty war. Very
nasty indeed."

Well, he looked like a frog, right enough. Short
and stubby, round spectacles with thick lenses that
made his eyes big. And his clothes *were* odd. Expensive, mind, you could see that. But his jacket seemed to
drape where there wasn't any room for drape. What did
surprise Rigby was his shyness. Rigby had expected
someone a little brash, a little too smooth for Carne,
whereas Smiley had an earnest formality of manner
which appealed to Rigby's conservative taste.

Smiley took the letter from his wallet and put it on
the desk, while Rigby extracted an old pair of gold-
rimmed spectacles from a battered metal case and adjusted the ends carefully over his ears.

"I don't know if Ben explained," said Smiley, "but
this letter was sent to the correspondence section of a
small Nonconformist journal to which Mrs. Rode subscribed."

"And Miss Fellowship is the lady who brought you
the letter?"

"No; her name is Brimley. She is the editor of the
magazine. Fellowship is just a pen-name for the correspondence column."

The brown eyes rested on him for a moment.

"When did she receive this letter?"

"Yesterday, the seventeenth. Thursday's the day
they go to press, their busy day. The afternoon mail
doesn't get opened till the evening, usually. This was
opened about six o'clock, I suppose."

"And she brought it straight to you?"

"Yes."

"Why?"

"She worked for me during the war, in my department. She was reluctant to go straight to the police—I
was the only person she could think of who wasn't a

policeman," he added stupidly. "Who could help, I mean."

"May I ask what you yourself, sir, do for a living?"

"Nothing much. A little private research on seventeenth-century Germany." It seemed a very silly answer.

Rigby didn't seem bothered.

"What's this earlier letter she talks about?"

Smiley offered him the second envelope, and again the big, square hand received it.

"It appears she won this competition," Smiley explained. "That was her winning entry. I gather she comes from a family which has subscribed to the magazine since its foundation. That's why Miss Brimley was less inclined to regard the letter as nonsense. Not that it follows."

"Not that what follows?"

"I meant that the fact that her family had subscribed to a journal for fifty years does not logically affect the possibility that she was unbalanced."

Rigby nodded, as if he saw the point, but Smiley had an uncomfortable feeling that he did not.

"Ah," said Rigby, with a slow smile. "Women, eh?"

Smiley, completely bewildered, gave a little laugh. Rigby was looking at him thoughtfully.

"Know any of the staff, here, do you, sir?"

"Only Mr. Terence Fielding. We met at an Oxford dinner some time ago. I thought I'd call round and see him. I knew his brother pretty well."

Rigby appeared to stiffen slightly at the mention of Fielding, but he said nothing, and Smiley went on:

"It was Fielding I rang when Miss Brimley brought me the letter. He told me the news. That was last night."

"I see."

They looked at one another again in silence. Smiley discomfited and slightly comic, Rigby appraising him, wondering how much to say.

"How long are you staying?" he said at last.

"I don't know," Smiley replied. "Miss Brimley wanted to come herself, but she has her paper to run. She attached great importance, you see, to doing all she could for Mrs. Rode, even though she was dead. Because she was a subscriber, I mean. I promised to see that the letter arrived quickly in the right hands. I don't imagine there's much else I can do. I shall probably stay on for a day or two just to have a word with Fielding . . . go to the funeral, I suppose. I've booked in at the Sawley Arms."

"Fine hotel, that."

Rigby put his spectacles carefully back into their case and dropped the case into a drawer.

"Funny place, Carne. There's a big gap between the Town and Gown, as we say; neither side knows nor likes the other. It's fear that does it, fear and ignorance. It makes it hard in a case like this. Oh, I can call on Mr. Fielding and Mr. D'Arcy and they say, 'Good day, Sergeant,' and give me a cup of tea in the kitchen, but I can't get among them. They've got their own community, see, and no one outside it can get in. No gossip in the pubs, no contacts, nothing . . . just cups of tea and bits of seed cake, and being called Sergeant." Rigby laughed suddenly, and Smiley with him in relief. "There's a lot I'd like to ask them, a lot of things; who liked the Rodes and who didn't, whether Mr. Rode's a good teacher and whether his wife fitted with the others. I've got all the facts I want, but I've got no clothes to hang on them." He looked at Smiley expectantly. There was a very long silence.

"If you want me to help, I'd be delighted," said Smiley at last. "But give me the facts first."

"Stella Rode was murdered between about ten past eleven and quarter to twelve on the night of Wednesday the sixteenth. She must have been struck fifteen to twenty times with a cosh or bit of piping or something. It was a terrible murder . . . terrible. There are marks all over her body. At a guess I would say she came from the drawing room to the front door to answer the bell or something, when she opened the door she was struck down and dragged to the conservatory. The conservatory door was unlocked, see?"

"I see. . . . It's odd that he should have known that, isn't it?"

"The murderer may have been hiding there already: we can't tell from the prints just there. He was wearing boots—wellington boots, size 10½. We would guess from the spacing of the footprints in the garden that he was about six foot tall. When he had got her to the conservatory he must have hit her again and again—mainly on the head. There's a lot of what we call travelled blood in the conservatory, that's to say, blood spurted from an open artery. There's no sign of that anywhere else."

"And no sign of it on her husband?"

"I'll come to that later, but the short answer is, no." He paused a moment and continued:

"Now, I said there were footprints, and so there were. The murderer came through the back garden. Where he came from and went to, Heaven alone knows. You see, there are no tracks leading away—not wellingtons. None at all. Of course, it's possible the outgoing tracks followed the path to the front gate and got lost in all the to-ing and fro-ing later that night. But I don't think we'd have lost them even then." He glanced at Smiley, then went on:

"He left one thing behind him in the conservatory—an old cloth belt, navy blue, from a cheap overcoat by the look of it. We're working on that now."

"Was she . . . robbed or anything?"

"No sign of interference. She was wearing a string of green beads round her neck, and they've gone, and it looks as though he tried to get the rings off her finger, but they were too tight." He paused.

"I need hardly tell you that we've had reports from every corner of the country about tall men in blue overcoats and gumboots. But none of them had wings as far as I know. Or seven-league boots for jumping from the conservatory to the road."

They paused, while a police cadet brought in tea on a tray. He put it on the desk, looked at Smiley out of the corner of his eye and decided to let the Inspector pour out. He guided the teapot round so that the handle was towards Rigby and withdrew. Smiley was amused by the immaculate condition of the tray cloth, by the matching china and the tea-strainer, laid before them by the enormous hands of the cadet. Rigby poured out the tea and they drank for a moment in silence. There was, Smiley reflected, something devastatingly competent about Rigby. The very ordinariness of the man and his room identified him with the society he protected. The nondescript furniture, the wooden filing cupboards, the bare walls, the archaic telephone with its separate ear-piece, the brown frieze round the wall and the brown paint on the door, the glistening linoleum and the faint smell of carbolic, the burbling gas-fire and the calendar from the Prudential—these were the evidence of recti-tude and moderation; their austerity gave comfort and reassurance. Rigby continued:

"Rode went back to Fielding's house for the exami-nation papers. Fielding confirms that, of course. He ar-rived at Fielding's house at about 11.35, near as Field-ing can say. He hardly spent any time there at all—just collected his papers at the door—they were in a small writing-case he uses for carrying exercise books. He doesn't remember whether he saw anyone on the road. He thinks a bicycle overtook him, but he can't be sure. If we take Rode's word for it, he walked straight home. When he got there he rang the bell. He was wearing a dinner jacket and so he hadn't got his key with him. His wife was expecting him to ring the bell, you see. That's the devil of it. It was a moonlit night, mind, and snow on the ground, so you could see a mighty long way. He called her, but she didn't answer. Then he saw the foot-prints going round to the side of the house. Not just footprints, but blood marks and the snow all churned up where the body had been dragged to the conserva-tory. But he didn't know it was blood in the moonlight, it just showed up dark, and Rode said afterwards he thought it was the dirty water from the gutters running over on to the path.

"He followed the prints round until he came to the conservatory. It was darker in there and he fumbled for the light switch, but it didn't work."

"Did he light a match?"

"No, he didn't have any. He's a non-smoker. His wife didn't approve of smoking. He moved forward from the door. The conservatory walls are mainly glass except for the bottom three feet, but the roof is tiled. The moon was high that night, and not much light got in at all, except through the partition window between the drawing room and the conservatory—but she'd only had the little table light on in the drawing-room. So he groped his way forward, talking all the time, calling Stella, his wife. As he went, he tripped over something and nearly fell. He knelt down and felt with his hands, up and down her body. He realised that his hands were covered in blood. He doesn't remember much after that, but there's a senior master living a hundred yards up the road—Mr. D'Arcy his name is, lives with his sister, and he heard him screaming on the road. D'Arcy went out to him. Rode had blood all over his hands and face and seemed to be out of his mind. D'Arcy rang the police and I got there at about one o'clock that morning. I've seen some nasty things in my time, but this is the worst. Blood everywhere. Whoever killed her must have been covered in it. There's an outside tap against the conservatory wall. The tap had been turned on, probably by the murderer to rinse his hands. The boffins have found traces of blood in the snow underneath it. The tap was lagged recently by Rode I gather. . . ."

"And fingerprints?" Smiley asked. "What about them?"

"Mr. Rode's were everywhere. On the floor, the walls and windows, on the body itself. But there were other prints; smudges of blood, little more, made with a gloved hand probably."

"And they were the murderer's?"

"They had been made *before* Rode made his. In some cases Rode's prints were partly superimposed on the glove prints."

Smiley was silent for a moment.

"These examination papers he went back for. Were they as important as all that?"

"Yes. I gather they were. Up to a point anyway. The marks had to be handed in to Mr. D'Arcy by midday on Friday."

"But why did he take them to Fielding's in the first place?"

"He didn't. He'd been invigilating exams all afternoon and the papers were handed in to him at six o'clock. He put them in his little case and had them taken to Fielding's by a boy—head boy in Mr. Fielding's house, name of Perkins. Rode was on Chapel duty last week, so he didn't have time to return home before dinner."

"Where did he change then?"

"In the Tutors' Robing Room, next to the Common Room. There are facilities there, mainly for games tutors who live some distance from Carne."

"The boy who brought this case to Fielding's house—who was he?"

"I can't tell you much more than I've said. His name is Perkins; he's head of Mr. Fielding's house. Fielding has spoken to him and confirmed Rode's statement. . . . House tutors are very possessive about their boys, you know . . . don't like them to be spoken to by rough policemen." Rigby seemed to be slightly upset.

"I see," Smiley said at last, helplessly, and then: "But how do you explain the letter?"

"It isn't only the letter we've got to explain."

Smiley looked at him sharply.

"What do you mean?"

"I mean," said Rigby slowly, "that Mrs. Rode did several pretty queer things in the last few weeks."

IV

Town And Gown

"Mrs. Rode was Chapel, of course," Rigby continued, "and we've quite a community in Carne. Truth to tell," he added with a slow smile, "my wife belongs to it.

"A couple of weeks ago our Minister called round to see me. It was in the evening, about half past six, I suppose. I was just thinking of going home, see. He walked in here and sat himself down where you're sitting now. He's a big fellow, the Minister, a fine man; comes from up North, where Mrs. Rode came from. Cardew, his name is."

"The Mr. Cardew in the letter?"

"That's him. He knew all about Mrs. Rode's family before the Rodes ever came here. Glaston's quite a name up North, and Mr. Cardew was very pleased when he heard that Stella Rode was Mr. Glaston's daughter; very pleased indeed. Mrs. Rode came to the Tabernacle regular as clockwork, you can imagine, and they like to see that round here. My wife was pleased as Punch, I can tell you. It was the first time, I suppose, that anyone from the School had done that. Most of the Chapel people here are tradespeople—what we call the locals." Rigby smiled again. "It isn't often that town and gown come together, so to speak. Not here."

"How about her husband? Was he Chapel too?"

"Well, he had been, so she told Mr. Cardew. Mr.

33

Rode was born and bred in Branxome, and all his family were Chapel people. That's how Mr. and Mrs. Rode first met, I gather—at Branxome Tabernacle. Ever been there, have you? A fine church Branxome, right up on the hill there, overlooking the sea."

Smiley shook his head and Rigby's wide brown eyes rested on him thoughtfully for a moment.

"You should," he said, "you should go and see that. It seems," he continued, "that Mr. Rode turned Church of England when he came to Carne. Even tried to persuade his wife to do the same. They're very strong at the School. I heard that from my wife, as a matter of fact. I never let her gossip as a rule, being a policeman's wife and that, but Mr. Cardew told her that himself."

"I see," said Smiley.

"Well now, Cardew came and saw me. He was all worried and bothered with himself. He didn't know what he should make of it, but he wanted to talk to me as a friend and not as a policeman." Rigby looked sour, "When people say that to me, I always know that they want to talk to me as a policeman. Then he told me his story. Mrs. Rode had called to see him that afternoon. He'd been out visiting a farmer's wife over in Okeford and didn't come home until half past five or thereabouts, so Mrs. Cardew had had to talk to her and hold the fort until the Minister came home. Mrs. Rode was white as a sheet, sitting very still by the fire. As soon as the Minister arrived, Mrs. Cardew left them alone and Stella Rode started talking about her husband."

He paused. "She said Mr. Rode was going to kill her. In the long nights. She seemed to have a kind of fixation about being murdered in the long nights. Cardew didn't take it too seriously at first, but thinking about it afterwards, he decided to let me know."

Smiley looked at him sharply.

"He couldn't make out what she meant. He thought she was out of her mind. He's a down-to-earth man, see, although he's a Minister. I think he was probably a bit too firm with her. He asked her what put this dreadful thought into her head, and she began to weep. Not hysterical, apparently, but just crying quietly to herself. He tried to calm her down, promised to help her any way he could, and asked her again what had given her this idea. She just shook her head, then got up, walked over to the door, still shaking her head in despair. She turned to him, and he thought she was going to say something, but she didn't. She just left."

"How very curious," said Smiley, "that she lied about that in her letter. She went out of her way to say she *hadn't* told Cardew."

Rigby shrugged his great shoulders.

"If you'll pardon me," he said, "I'm in a darned awkward position. The Chief Constable would sooner cut his throat than call in Scotland Yard. He wants an arrest and he wants one quick. We've got enough clues to cover a Christmas tree; footprints, time of the murder, indication of murderer's clothing and even the weapon itself."

Smiley looked at him in surprise.

"You've *found* the weapon, then?"

Rigby hesitated. "Yes, we've found it. There's hardly a soul knows this, sir, and I'll trouble you to remember that. We found it the morning after the murder, four miles north of Carne on the Okeford road, tossed into a ditch. Eighteen inches of what they call coaxial cable. Know what that is, do you? It comes in all sizes, but this piece is about two inches in diameter. It has a copper rod running down the middle and the plastic insulation between the rod and the outer cover. There was blood on it: Stella Rode's blood group, and hairs from her head, stuck to the blood. We're keeping that very dark indeed. By the Grace of God, it was found by one of our own men. It pinpoints the line of the murderer's departure."

"There's no doubt, I suppose, that it *is* the weapon?" Smiley asked lamely.

"We found particles of copper in the wounds on the body."

"It's odd, isn't it," Smiley suggested reflectively, "that the murderer should have carried the weapon so far before getting rid of it? Specially if he was walking.

You'd think he'd want to get rid of it as soon as he could."

"It is odd. Very odd. The Okeford road runs beside the canal for half of those four miles; he could have pitched the cable into the canal anywhere along there. We'd never have been the wiser."

"Was the cable old?"

"Not particularly. Just standard type. It could have come from almost anywhere." Rigby hesitated a minute, then burst out:

"Look, sir, this is what I am trying to say. The circumstances of this case demand a certain type of investigation: wide-scale search, detailed laboratory work, mass enquiry. That's what the Chief wants, and he's right. We've no case against the husband at all, and to be frank he's precious little use to us. He seems a bit lost, a bit vague, contradicting himself on little things that don't matter, like the date of his marriage or the name of his doctor. It's shock, of course, I've seen it before. I know all about your letter, sir, and it's damned odd, but if you can tell me how he could have produced wellington boots out of a hat and got rid of them afterwards, battered his wife to death without leaving more than a few smudges of blood on himself, and got the weapon four miles from the scene of the crime, all within ten minutes of being at Fielding's house, I'll be grateful to you. We're looking for a stranger, six foot tall, wearing newish Dunlop Wellington boots size 10½, leather gloves and an old blue overcoat stained with blood. A man who travels on foot, who was in the area of North Fields between 11.10 and 11.45 on the night of the murder, who left in the direction of Okeford, taking with him one and a half feet of coaxial cable, a string of green beads and an imitation diamond clip, valued at twenty-three and six. We're looking for a maniac, a man who kills for pleasure or the price of a meal." Rigby paused, smiled wistfully and added, "Who can fly fifty feet through the air. But with information like this how else should we spend our time? What else can we look for? I can't put men on to chasing shadows when there's work like that to be done."

"I understand that."

"But I'm an old policeman, Mr. Smiley, and I like to know what I'm about. I don't like looking for people I can't believe in, and I don't like being cut off from witnesses. I like to meet people and talk to them, nose about here and there, get to know the country. But I can't do that, not at the school. Do you follow me? So we've got to rely on laboratories, tracker dogs and nationwide searches, but somehow in my bones I don't think it's altogether one of those cases."

"I read in the paper about a woman, a Mad Janie . . ."

"I'm coming to that. Mrs. Rode was a kindly woman, easy to talk to. I always found her so, anyway. Some of the women at Chapel took against her, but you know what women are. It seems she got friendly with this Janie creature. Janie came begging, selling herbs and charms at the back door; you know the kind of thing. She's queer, talks to birds and all that. She lives in a disused Norman chapel over to Pylle. Stella Rode used to give her food and clothes—the poor soul was often as not half-starved. Now Janie's disappeared. She was seen early Wednesday night on the lane towards North Fields and hasn't been seen since. That don't mean a thing. These people come and go in their own way. They'll be all over the neighbourhood for years, then one day they're gone like snow in the fire. They've died in a ditch, maybe, or they've took ill and crept away like a cat. Janie's not the only queer one round here. There's a lot of excitement because we found a spare set of footprints running along the fringe of trees at the far end of the garden. They were a woman's prints by the look of them, and at one point they come quite close to the conservatory. Could be a gypsy or a beggar woman. Could be anything, but I expect it's Janie right enough. I hope to Heaven it was, sir; we could do with an eyewitness, even a mad one."

Smiley stood up. As they shook hands, Rigby said, "Goodbye, sir. Ring me any time, any time at all." He scribbled a telephone number on the pad in front of him, tore off the sheet and gave it to Smiley. "That's my home number." He showed Smiley to the door, seemed to hesitate, then he said, "You're not a Carnian yourself by any chance, are you, sir?"

"Good heavens, no."

Again Rigby hesitated. "Our Chief's a Carnian. Ex-Indian Army. Brigadier Havelock. This is his last year. He's very interested in this case. Doesn't like me messing around the school. Won't have it."

"I see."

"He wants an arrest quickly."

"And outside Carne, I suppose?"

"Goodbye, Mr. Smiley. Don't forget to ring me. Oh, another thing I should have mentioned. That bit of cable . . ."

"Yes?"

"Mr. Rode used a length of the same stuff in a demonstration lecture on elementary electronics. Mislaid it about three weeks ago."

Smiley walked slowly back to his hotel.

My dear Brim,

As soon as I arrived I handed your letter over to the C.I.D. man in charge of the case—it was Rigby, as Ben had supposed; he looks like a mixture of Humpty-Dumpty and a Cornish elf— very short and broad—and I don't think he's anyone's fool.

To begin at the middle—our letter didn't have quite the effect we expected; Stella Rode evidently told Cardew, the local Baptist Minister, two weeks ago, that her husband was trying to kill her in the long nights, whatever they are. As for the circumstances of the murder—the account in the Guardian is substantially correct.

In fact, the more Rigby told me, the less likely it became that she was killed by her husband. Almost everything pointed away from him. Quite apart from motive, there is the location of the weapon, the footprints in the snow (which indicate a tall man in wellingtons), the presence of unidentified glove-prints in the conservatory. Add to that the strongest argument of all: whoever killed her must have been covered in blood—the conservatory was a dreadful sight, Rigby tells me. Of course, there was blood on Rode when he was picked up by his colleague in the lane, but only smears which could have resulted from stumbling over the body in the dark. Incidentally, the foot-prints only go into the garden and not out.

As things stand at the moment, there is, as Rigby points out, only one interpretation—the murderer was a stranger, a tramp, a madman per-haps, who killed her for pleasure or for her jewel-ery (which was worthless) and made off along the Okeford road, throwing the weapon into a ditch. (But why carry it four miles—and why not throw it into the canal the other side of the ditch? The Okeford road crosses Okemoor, which is all cross-dyked to prevent flooding.) If this interpretation is correct, then I suppose we attribute Stella's let-ter and her interview with Cardew to a persecuted mind, or the premonition of death, depending on whether we're superstitious. If that is so, it is the most monstrous coincidence I have ever heard of. Which brings me to my final point.

I rather gathered from what Rigby didn't say that his Chief Constable was treading on his tail, urging him to scour the country for tramps in bloodstained blue overcoats (you remember the belt). Rigby, of course, has no alternative but to follow the signs and do as his Chief expects—but he is clearly uneasy about something—either something he hasn't told me, or something he just feels in his bones. I think he was sincere when he asked me to tell him anything I found out about the School end—the Rodes themselves, the way they fitted in, and so on. Carne's monastery walls are still pretty high, he feels. . . .

So I'll just sniff around a bit, I think, and see what goes on. I rang Fielding when I got back from the police station and he's asked me to sup-per tonight. I'll write again as soon as I have any-thing to tell you.

George.

Having carefully sealed the envelope, pressing down the corners with his thumbs, Smiley locked his door and made his way down the wide marble staircase, treading carefully on the meagre coconut matting that ran down the centre. There was a red wooden letter box in the hall for the use of residents, but Smiley, being a cautious man, avoided it. He walked to the pillar box at the corner of the road, posted his letter and wondered what to do about lunch. There were, of course, the sandwiches and coffee provided by Miss Brimley. Reluctantly he returned to the hotel. It was full of journalists, and Smiley hated journalists. It was also cold, and he hated the cold. And there was something very familiar about sandwiches in a hotel bedroom.

V

Cat And Dog

It was just after seven o'clock that evening when George Smiley climbed the steps which led up to the front door of Mr. Terence Fielding's house. He rang, and was admitted to the hall by a little plump woman in her middle fifties. To his right a log fire burned warmly on a pile of wood ash and above him he was vaguely aware of a minstrel gallery and a mahogany staircase, which rose in a spiral to the top of the house. Most of the light seemed to come from the fire, and Smiley could see that the walls around him were hung with a great number of paintings of various styles and periods, and the chimney-piece was laden with all manner of *objets d'art*. With an involuntary shudder, he noticed that neither the fire nor the pictures quite succeeded in banishing the faint smell of school—of polish bought wholesale, of cocoa and community cooking. Corridors led from the hall, and Smiley observed that the lower part of each wall was painted a dark brown or green according to the inflexible rule of school decorators. From one of these corridors the enormous figure of Mr. Terence Fielding emerged.

He advanced on Smiley, massive and genial, with his splendid mane of grey hair falling anyhow across his forehead, and his gown billowing behind him.

"Smiley? Ah! You've met True, have you—Miss

Truebody, my housekeeper? Marvellous this snow, isn't it? Pure Breughel! Seen the boys skating by the Eyot? Marvellous sight! Black suits, coloured scarves, pale sun; all there, isn't it, all there! Breughel to the life. Marvellous!" He took Smiley's coat and flung it on to a decrepit deal chair with a rush seat which stood in the corner of the hall.

"You like that chair—you recognise it?"

"I don't think I do," Smiley replied in some confusion.

"Ah, you should, you know, you should! Had it made in Provence before the war. Little carpenter I knew. Place it now? Facsimile of Van Gogh's yellow chair; some people recognise it." He led the way down a corridor and into a large comfortable study adorned with Dutch tiles, small pieces of Renaissance sculpture, mysterious bronzes, china dogs and unglazed vases; and Fielding himself towering magnificent among them.

As senior housemaster of Carne, Fielding wore, in place of the customary academic dress, a wonderful confection of heavy black skirts and legal bib, like a monk in evening dress. All this imparted a suggestion of clerical austerity in noted contrast to the studied flamboyance of his personality. Evidently conscious of this, he sought to punctuate the solemnity of his uniform and give to it a little of his own temperament, by adorning it with flowers carefully chosen from his garden. He had scandalised the tailors of Carne, whose frosted windows carried the insignia of royal households, by having buttonholes let into his gown. These he would fill according to his mood with anything from hibernia to bluebells. This evening he wore a rose, and from its freshness Smiley deduced that he had this minute put it into place, having ordered it specially.

"Sherry wine or Madeira?"

"Thank you; a glass of sherry."

"Tart's drink, Madeira," Fielding called, as he poured from a decanter, "but boys like it. Perhaps that's why. They're frightful flirts." He handed Smiley a glass and added, with a dramatic modification of his voice:

"We're all rather subdued at the moment by this

dreadful business. We've never had anything quite like it, you know. Have you seen the evening papers?"

"No, I'm afraid I haven't. But the Sawley Arms is packed with journalists of course."

"They've really gone to town. They've got the Army out in Hampshire, playing about with mine-detectors. God knows what they expect to find."

"How have the boys taken it?"

"They adore it! My own house has been particularly fortunate, of course, because the Rodes were dining here that night. Some oaf from the police even wanted to question one of my boys."

"Indeed," said Smiley innocently. "What on earth about?"

"Oh, God knows," Fielding replied abruptly, and then, changing the subject, he asked, "You knew my brother well, didn't you? He talked about you, you know."

"Yes, I knew Adrian very well. We were close friends."

"In the war, too?"

"Yes."

"Were you in his crowd, then?"

"What crowd?"

"Steed, Asprey, Jebedee. All those people."

"Yes."

"I never really heard how he died. Did you?"

"No."

"We didn't see much of one another in later years, Adrian and I. Being a fraud, I can't afford to be seen beside the genuine article," Fielding declared, with something of his earlier panache. Smiley was spared the embarrassment of a reply by a quiet knock at the door, and a tall red-haired boy came timidly into the room.

"I've called the Adsum, sir, if you're ready, sir."

"Damn," said Fielding, emptying his glass. "Prayers." He turned to Smiley.

"Meet Perkins, my head prefect. Musical genius, but a problem in the schoolroom. That right, Tim? Stay here or come as you like. It only lasts ten minutes."

"Rather less tonight, sir," said Perkins. "It's the Nunc Dimittis."

"Thank God for small mercies," Fielding declared, tugging briefly at his bib, as he led Smiley at a spanking pace out into the corridor and across the hall, with Perkins stalking along behind them. Fielding was speaking all the time without bothering to turn his head:

"I'm glad you've chosen this evening to come. I never entertain on Saturdays as a rule because everyone else does, though none of us quite knows what to do about entertaining at the moment. Felix D'Arcy will be coming tonight, but that's hardly entertaining. D'Arcy's a professional. Incidentally, we normally dress in the evening, but it doesn't matter."

Smiley's heart sank. They turned a corner and entered another corridor.

"We have prayers at all hours here. The Master's revived the seven Day Hours for the Offices: Prime, Terce, Sext and so on. A surfeit during the Half, abstinence during the holidays, that's the system, like games. Useful in the house for roll-calls, too." He led the way down yet another corridor, flung open a double door at the end of it and marched straight into the dining-room, his gown filling gracefully behind him. The boys were waiting for him.

"More sherry? What did you think of prayers? They sing quite nicely, don't they? One or two good tenors. We tried some plainsong last Half; quite good, really quite good. D'Arcy will be here soon. He's a frightful toad. Looks like a Sickert model fifty years after—all trousers and collar. However, you're lucky his sister isn't accompanying him. She's worse!"

"What's his subject?" They were back in Fielding's study.

"Subject! I'm afraid we don't have subjects here. None of us has read a word on any subject since we left University." He lowered his voice and added darkly, "That's if we *went* to University. D'Arcy teaches French. D'Arcy is senior tutor by election, bachelor by profession, sublimated pansy by inclination . . ." he was standing quite still now, his head thrown back and his right hand stretched out towards Smiley, ". . . and his subject is other people's shortcomings. He is principally, however, self-appointed majordomo of Carne protocol. If you wear a gown on a bicycle, reply incorrectly to an invitation, make a fault in the *placement* of your dinner guests or speak of a colleague as 'Mister,' D'Arcy will find you out and admonish you."

"What are the duties of Senior Tutor, then?" Smiley asked, just for something to say.

"He's the referee between the classics and the scientists; arranges the timetable and vets the exam. results. But principally, poor man, he must reconcile the Arts with the Sciences." He shook his head sagely. "And it takes a better man than D'Arcy to do that. Not, mind you," he added wearily, "that it makes the least difference who wins the extra hour on Friday evenings. Who cares? Not the boys, poor dears, that's certain."

Fielding talked on, at random and always in superlatives, sometimes groping in the air with his hand as if to catch the more elusive metaphors; now of his colleagues with caustic derision, now of boys with compassion if not with understanding; now of the Arts with fervour—and the studied bewilderment of a lonely disciple.

"Carne isn't a school. It's a sanatorium for intellectual lepers. The symptoms began when we came down from University; a gradual putrefication of our intellectual extremities. From day to day our minds die, our spirits atrophy and rot. We watch the process in one another, hoping to forget it in ourselves." He paused, and looked reflectively at his hands.

"In me the process is complete. You see before you a dead soul, and Carne is the body I live in." Much pleased by this confession, Fielding held out his great arms so that the sleeves of his gown resembled the wings of a giant bat, "the Vampire of Carne," he declared, bowing deeply. "Alcoholique et poete!" A bellow of laughter followed this display.

Smiley was fascinated by Fielding, by his size, his voice, the wanton inconstancy of his temperament, by his whole big-screen style; he found himself attracted and repelled by this succession of contradictory poses; he wondered whether he was supposed to take part in the performance, but Fielding seemed so dazzled by the footlights that he was indifferent to the audience behind them. The more Smiley watched, the more elusive seemed the character he was trying to comprehend: changeful but sterile, daring but fugitive; colourful, unbounded, ingenuous, yet deceitful and perverse. Smiley began to wish he could acquire the material facts of Fielding—his means, his ambitions and disappointments.

His reverie was interrupted by Miss Truebody. Felix D'Arcy had arrived.

No candles, and a cold supper admirably done by Miss Truebody. Not claret, but hock, passed round like port. And at last, at long last, Fielding mentioned Stella Rode.

They had been talking rather dutifully of the Arts and the Sciences. This would have been dull (for it was uninformed) had not D'Arcy constantly been goaded by Fielding, who seemed anxious to exhibit D'Arcy in his worst light. D'Arcy's judgements of people and problems were largely coloured by what he considered "seemly" (a favourite word) and by an effeminate malice towards his colleagues. After a while Fielding asked who was replacing Rode during his absence, to which D'Arcy said, "No one," and added unctuously:

"It was a terrible shock to the community, this affair."

"Nonsense," Fielding retorted. "Boys love disaster. The further we are from death the more attractive it seems. They find the whole affair most exhilarating."

"The publicity has been most unseemly," said D'Arcy, "most. I think that has been prominent in the minds of many of us in the Common Room." He turned to Smiley:

"The press, you know, is a constant worry here. In the past it could never have happened. Formerly our great families and institutions were not subjected to this intrusion. No, indeed not. But today all that is changed. Many of us are compelled to subscribe to the cheaper newspapers for this very reason. One Sunday newspaper mentioned no fewer than four of Hecht's old boys in one edition. All of them in an unseemly context, I may say. And of course such papers never fail to mention that the boy is a Carnian. You know, I suppose, that we have the young prince here. (I myself have the honour to supervise his French studies.) The young Sawley is also at Carne. The activity of the press during his parents' divorce suit was deplorable. Quite deplorable. The Master wrote to the Press Council, you know. I drafted the letter myself. But on this tragic occasion they have excelled themselves. We even had the press at Compline last night, you know, waiting for the Special Prayer. They occupied the whole of the two rear pews on the west side. Hecht was doing Chapel Duty and tried to have them removed." He paused, raised his eyebrows in gentle reproach and smiled. "He had no business to, of course, but that never stopped the good Hecht." He turned to Smiley. "One of our *athletic* brethren," he explained.

"Stella was too common for you, Felix, wasn't she?"

"Not at all," said D'Arcy quickly. "I would not have you say that of me, Terence. I am by no means discriminatory in the matter of class; merely of manners. I grant you, in that particular field, I found her wanting."

.. "In many ways she was just what we needed," Fielding continued, addressing Smiley and ignoring D'Arcy. "She was everything we're forced to ignore—she was red-brick, council estates, new towns, the very antithesis of Carne!" He turned suddenly to D'Arcy and said, "But to you, Felix, she was just bad form."

"Not at all; merely unsuitable."

Fielding turned to Smiley in despair.

"Look," he said. "We talk academic here, you know, wear academic dress and hold high table dinners in the Common Room; we have long graces in Latin that none of us can translate. We go to the Abbey and the wives sit in the hencoop in their awful hats. But it's a charade. It means nothing."

D'Arcy smiled wanly.

"I cannot believe, my dear Terence, that anyone who keeps such an excellent table as yourself can have so low an opinion of the refinements of social conduct." He looked to Smiley for support and Smiley dutifully echoed the compliment. "Besides, we know Terence of old at Carne. I am afraid we are accustomed to his roar."

"I know why you disliked that woman, Felix. She was honest, and Carne has no defence against that kind of honesty."

D'Arcy suddenly became very angry indeed.

"Terence, I will not have you say this. I simply will not have it. I feel I have a certain duty at Carne, as indeed we all have, to restore and maintain those standards of behaviour which suffered so sadly in the war. I am sensible that this determination has made me on more than one occasion unpopular. But such comment or advice as I offer is never—I beg you to notice this—is *never* directed against personalities, only against behaviour, against unseemly lapses in conduct. I will acknowledge that more than once I was compelled to address Rode on the subject of his wife's conduct. That is a matter quite divorced from personalities, Terence. I will not have it said that I disliked Mrs. Rode. Such a suggestion would be disagreeable at all times, but under the present tragic circumstances it is deplorable. Mrs. Rode's own . . . background and education did not naturally prepare her for our ways; that is quite a different matter. It does, however, illustrate the point that I wish to emphasise, Terence: it was a question of enlightenment, not of criticism. Do I make myself clear?"

"Abundantly," Fielding answered drily.

"Did the other wives like her?" Smiley ventured.

"Not entirely," D'arcy replied crisply.

"The wives! My God!" Fielding groaned, putting his hand to his brow. There was a pause.

"Her clothes, I believe, were a source of distress to some of them. She also frequented the public laundry.

This, too, would not make a favourable impression. I should add that she did not attend our church. . . ."

"Did she have any close friends among the wives?" Smiley persisted.

"I believe young Mrs. Snow took to her."

"And you say she was dining here the night she was murdered?"

"Yes," said Fielding quietly, "Wednesday. And it was Felix and his sister who took in poor Rode afterwards. . . ." He glanced at D'Arcy.

"Yes, indeed," said D'Arcy abruptly. His eyes were on Fielding, and it seemed to Smiley that something had passed between them. "We shall never forget, never. . . . Terence, if I may talk shop for just one moment, Perkins' construe is abysmal; I declare I have never seen work like it. Is he unwell? His mother is a most cultured woman, a cousin of the Samfords, I am told."

Smiley looked at him and wondered. His dinner jacket was faded, green with age. Smiley could almost hear him saying it had belonged to his grandfather. The skin of his face was so unlined that he somehow suggested fatness without being fat. His voice was pitched on one insinuating note, and he smiled all the time, whether he was speaking or not. The smile never left his smooth face, it was worked into the malleable fabric of his flesh, stretching his lips across his perfect teeth and opening the corners of his red mouth, so that it seemed to be held in place by the invisible fingers of his dentist. Yet D'Arcy's face was far from unexpressive; every mark showed. The smallest movement of his mouth or nose, the quickest glance or frown, were there to read and interpret. And he wanted to change the subject. Not away from Stella Rode (for he returned to discussing her himself a moment later), but away from the particular evening on which she died, away from the precise narration of events. And what was more, there was not a doubt in Smiley's mind that Fielding had seen it too, that in that look which passed between them was a pact of fear, a warning perhaps, so that from that moment

Fielding's manner changed, he grew sullen and preoccupied, in a way that puzzled Smiley long afterwards.

D'Arcy turned to Smiley and addressed him with cloying intimacy.

"*Do* forgive my deplorable descent into Carne gossip. You find us a little cut off, here, do you not? We are often held to be cut off, I know. Carne is a 'Snob School,' that is the cry. You may read it every day in the gutter press. And yet, despite the claims of the *avant-garde*," he said, glancing slyly at Fielding, "I may say that *no one* could be less of a snob than Felix D'Arcy." Smiley noticed his hair. It was very fine and ginger, growing from the top and leaving his pink neck bare.

"Take poor Rode, for instance. I certainly don't hold Rode's background against him in any way, poor fellow. The grammar schools do a splendid job, I am sure. Besides, he settled down here very well. I told the Master so. I said to him that Rode had settled down well; he does Chapel duty quite admirably—that was the very point I made. I hope I have played my part, what is more, in helping him to fit in. With careful instruction, such people can, as I said to the Master, learn our customs and even our manners; and the Master agreed."

Smiley's glass was empty and D'Arcy, without consulting Fielding, filled it for him from the decanter. His hands were polished and hairless, like the hands of a girl.

"But," he continued, "I must be honest. Mrs. Rode did not adapt herself so willingly to our ways." Still smiling, he sipped delicately from his glass. He wants to put the record straight, thought Smiley.

"She would never really have fitted in at Carne; that is my opinion—though I am sure I never voiced it while she was alive. Her background was against her. The fault was not hers—it was her background which, as I say, was unfortunate. Indeed, if we may speak frankly and in confidence, I have reason to believe it was her past that brought about her death."

"Why do you say that?" asked Smiley quickly, and D'Arcy replied with a glance at Fielding, "It appears she was expecting to be attacked."

"My sister is devoted to dogs," D'Arcy continued. "You may know that already perhaps. King Charles spaniels are her *forte*. She took a first at the North Dorset last year and was commended at Cruft's shortly afterwards for her 'Queen of Carne.' She sells to America, you know. I dare say there are few people in the country with Dorothy's knowledge of the breed. The Master's wife found occasion to say the very same thing a week ago. Well, the Rodes were our neighbours, as you know, and Dorothy is not a person to neglect her neighbourly duties. Where duty is concerned, you will not find her discriminatory, I assure you. The Rodes also had a dog, a large mongrel, quite an intelligent animal, which they brought with them. (I have little idea where they came from, but that is another matter.) They appeared quite devoted to the dog, and I have no doubt they were. Rode took it with him to watch the football until I had occasion to advise him against it. The practice was giving rise to unseemly humour among the boys. I have found the same thing myself when exercising Dorothy's spaniels.

"I shall come to the point presently. Dorothy uses a vet called Harriman, a superior type of person who lives over toward Sturminster. A fortnight ago she sent for him. 'Queen of Carne' was coughing badly and Dorothy asked Harriman to come over. A bitch of her quality is not to be taken lightly, I assure you."

Fielding groaned, and D'Arcy continued, oblivious:

"I happened to be at home, and Harriman stayed for a cup of coffee. He is, as I say, a superior type of person. Harriman made some reference to the Rodes' dog and then the truth came out; Mrs. Rode had had the dog destroyed the previous day. She said it had bitten the postman. Some long and confused story; the Post Office would sue, the police had been round and I don't know what else. And, anyway, she said, the dog couldn't really protect, it could only warn. She had said so to Harriman, 'It wouldn't do any good.' "

"Wasn't she upset about losing the dog?" asked Smiley.

"Oh, indeed, yes. Harriman said she was in tears when she arrived. Mrs. Harriman had to give her a cup of tea. They suggested she should give the dog another chance, put it in kennels for a while, but she was adamant, quite adamant. Harriman was most perplexed. So was his wife. When they discussed it afterwards they agreed that Mrs. Rode's behaviour had not been quite normal. Not normal at all, in fact. Another curious fact was the condition of the dog: it had been maltreated, seriously so. Its back was marked as if from beatings."

"Did Harriman follow up this remark she made? About not doing any good? What did Harriman make of it?" Smiley was watching D'Arcy intently.

"She repeated it to Mrs. Harriman, but she wouldn't explain it. However, I think the explanation is obvious enough."

"Oh?" said Fielding.

D'Arcy put his head on one side and plucked coyly at the lobe of his ear.

"We all have a little of the detective in us," he said. "Dorothy and I talked it over after the—death. We decided that Stella Rode had formed some unsavoury association before coming to Carne, which had recently been revived . . . possibly against her will. Some violent ruffian—an old admirer—who would resent the improvement in her station."

"How badly was the postman bitten by the dog?" Smiley asked.

D'Arcy turned to him again.

"That is the extraordinary thing. That is the very crux of the story, my dear fellow: the postman hadn't been bitten at all. Dorothy enquired. Her whole story was an absolute string of lies from beginning to end."

They rose from the table and made their way to Fielding's study, where Miss Truebody had put the coffee. The conversation continued to wander back and forth over Wednesday's tragedy. D'Arcy was obsessed with the indelicacy of it all—the persistence of journalists, the insensitivity of the police, the uncertainty of Mrs. Rode's origin, the misfortune of her husband. Fielding was still oddly silent, sunk in his own thoughts, from which he occasionally emerged to glance at D'Arcy with a look of hostility. At exactly a quarter to eleven D'Arcy pronounced himself tired, and the three of them went into the great hall, where Miss Truebody produced a coat for Smiley and a coat and muffler and cap for D'Arcy. Fielding accepted D'Arcy's thanks with a sullen nod. He turned to Smiley:

"That business you rang me about. What was it exactly?"

"Oh—a letter from Mrs. Rode just before she was murdered," said Smiley vaguely, "the police are handling it now, but they do not regard it as . . . significant. Not significant at all. She seems to have had a sort of"—he gave an embarrassed grin—"persecution complex. Is that the expression? However, we might discuss it some time. You must dine with me at the Sawley before I go back. Do you come to London at all? We might meet in London perhaps, at the end of the Half."

D'Arcy was standing in the doorway, looking at the new fall of snow which lay white and perfect on the pavement before him.

"Ah," he said, with a little knowing laugh, "the long nights, eh, Terence, the long nights."

VI

Holly For The Devil

"What are the long nights?" Smiley asked, as he and D'Arcy walked briskly away from Fielding's house through the new snow towards the Abbey Close.

"We have a proverb that it always snows at Carne in the long nights. That is the traditional term here for the nights of Lent," D'Arcy replied. "Before the Reformation the monks of the Abbey kept a vigil during Lent between the Offices of Compline and Lauds. You may know that already perhaps. As there is no longer a religious order attached to the Abbey, the custom has fallen into disuse. We continue to observe it, however, by the saying of Compline during Lent. Compline was the last of the Canonical Day Hours and was said before retiring for the night. The Master, who has a great respect for traditions of this kind, has reintroduced the old words for our devotions. Prime was the dawn Office, as you are no doubt aware. Terce was at the third hour of daylight—that is to say at 9.0 a.m. Thus we no longer refer to Morning Prayer, but to Terce. I find it delightful. Similarly, during Advent and Lent we say Sext at midday in the Abbey."

"Are all these services compulsory?"

"Of course. Otherwise it would be necessary to make arrangements for those boys who did not attend.

That is not desirable. Besides, you forget that Carne is a religious foundation."

It was a beautiful night. As they crossed the Close, Smiley looked up at the tower. It seemed smaller and more peaceful in the moonlight. The whiteness of the new snow lit the very sky itself; the whole Abbey was so sharply visible against it that even the mutilated images of saints were clear in every sad detail of their deface-ment, wretched figures, their purpose lost, with no eyes to see the changing world.

They reached the cross-roads to the south of the Abbey.

"The parting of the ways, I fear," said D'Arcy, ex-tending his hand.

"It's a beautiful night," Smiley replied quickly, "let me come with you as far as your house."

"Gladly," said D'Arcy drily.

They turned down North Fields Lane. A high stone wall ran along one side; and on the other the great expanse of playing fields, twenty or more rugby pitches, bordered the road for over half a mile. They walked this distance in silence, until D'Arcy stopped and pointed with his stick past Smiley towards a small house on the edge of the playing fields.

"That's North Fields, the Rodes' house. It used to belong to the head groundsman, but the school added a wing a few years ago, and now it's a staff house. My own house is rather larger, and lies further up the road. Happily, I am fond of walking."

"Was it along here that you found Stanley Rode that night?"

There was a pause, then D'Arcy said: "It was nearer to my house, about a quarter of a mile further on. He was in a terrible condition, poor fellow, terrible. I am myself unable to bear the sight of blood. If I had known how he would look when I brought him into the house, I do not think I could have done it. Mercifully, my sister Dorothy is a most competent woman."

They walked on in silence, until Smiley said: "From what you were saying at dinner, the Rodes were a very ill-assorted couple."

"Precisely. If her death had happened any other way, I would describe it as providential: a blessed release for Rode. She was a thoroughly mischievous woman, Smiley, who made it her business to hold her husband up to ridicule. I believe it was intentional. Others do not. I do, and I have my reasons. She took pleasure in deriding her husband."

"And Carne too, no doubt."

"Just so. This is a critical moment in Carne's development. Many Public Schools have conceded to the vulgar clamour for change—change at any price. Carne, I am pleased to say, has not joined these Gadarene swine. That makes it more important than ever that we protect ourselves from within as well as from without." He spoke with surprising vehemence.

"But was she really such a problem? Surely her husband could have spoken to her?"

"I never encouraged him to do so, I assure you. It is not my practice to interfere between man and wife."

They reached D'Arcy's house. A high laurel hedge entirely concealed the house from the road, except for two multiple chimney-stacks which were visible over the top of it, confirming Smiley's impression that the house was large and Victorian.

"I am not ashamed of the Victorian taste," said D'Arcy as he slowly opened the gate; "but then, I am afraid we are not close to the modern idiom at Carne. This house used to be the rectory for North Fields Church, but the church is now served by a priest-in-charge from the Abbey. The vicarage is still within the school's gift, and I was fortunate enough to receive it. Good night. You must come for sherry before you go. Do you stay long?"

"I doubt it," Smiley replied, "but I am sure you have enough worries at the moment."

"What do you mean?" D'Arcy said sharply.

"The press, the police and all the attendant fuss."

"Ah yes, just so. Quite so. Nevertheless, our community life must continue. We always have a small party in the middle of the Half, and I feel it is particularly important that we should do so on this occasion. I will send a note to the Sawley tomorrow. My sister would be charmed. Good night." He clanged the gate to, and the sound was greeted by the frantic barking of dogs from somewhere behind the house. A window opened and a harsh female voice called:

"Is that you, Felix?"

"Yes, Dorothy."

"Why do you have to make such a bloody noise? You've woken those dogs again." The window closed with a significant thud, and D'Arcy, without so much as a glance in Smiley's direction, disappeared quickly into the shadow of the house.

Smiley set off along the road again, back towards the town. After walking for about ten minutes he stopped and looked again towards the Rodes' house a hundred yards across the playing fields. It lay in the shadow of a small coppice of fir trees, dark and secret against the white fields. A narrow lane led towards the house; there was a brick pillar-box on one corner and a small oak sign-post, quite new, pointed along the lane, which must, he decided, lead to the village of Pylle. The legend upon the sign was obscured by a film of snow, and Smiley brushed it away with his hand, so that he could read the words "North Fields," done in a contrived suburban Gothic script which must have caused D'Arcy considerable discomfort. The snow in the lane was untrodden; obviously more had fallen recently. There could not be much traffic between Pylle and Carne. Glancing quickly up and down the main road he began making his way along the lane. The hedge rose high on either side, and soon Smiley could see nothing but the pale sky above him, and the straggling willow wands reaching towards it. Once he thought he heard the sound of a footstep close behind him, but when he stopped he heard nothing but the furtive rustle of the laden hedges. He grew more conscious of the cold: it seemed to hang in the still damp of the sunken road, to clutch and hold him like the chill air of an empty house. Soon the hedge on his left gave way to a sparse line of trees, which Smiley judged to belong to the coppice he had seen from the road. The snow beneath the trees was patchy, and the bare ground looked suddenly ugly and torn. The lane took him in a gradual curve to the left and, quite suddenly the house stood before him, gaunt and craggy in the moonlight. The walls were brick and flint, half obscured by the mass of ivy which grew in profusion across them, tumbling over the porch in a tangled mane.

He glanced towards the garden. The coppice which bordered the lane encroached almost as far as the corner of the house, and extended to the far end of the lawn, screening the house from the playing fields. The murderer had reached the house by a path which led across the lawn and through the trees to the lane at the furthest end of the garden. Looking carefully at the snow on the lawn, he was able to discern the course of the path. The white glazed door to the left of the house must lead to the conservatory . . . And suddenly he knew he was afraid—afraid of the house, afraid of the sprawling dark garden. The knowledge came to him like an awareness of pain. The ivy walls seemed to reach forward and hold him, like an old woman cosseting an unwilling child. The house was large, yet dingy, holding to itself unearthly shapes, black and oily in the sudden contrasts of moonlight. Fascinated despite his fear, he moved towards it. The shadows broke and reformed, darting swiftly and becoming still, hiding in the abundant ivy, or merging with the black windows.

He observed in alarm the first involuntary movement of panic. He was afraid, then suddenly the senses joined in one concerted cry of terror, where sight and sound and touch could no longer be distinguished in the frenzy of his brain. He turned round and ran back to the gate. As he did so, he looked over his shoulder towards the house.

A woman was standing in the path, looking at him, and behind her the conservatory door swung slowly on its hinges.

For a second she stood quite still, then turned and ran back towards the conservatory. Forgetting his fear,

Smiley followed. As he reached the corner of the house he saw to his astonishment that she was standing at the door, rocking it gently back and forth in a thoughtful, leisurely way, like a child. She had her back to Smiley, until suddenly she turned to him and spoke, with a soft Dorset drawl, and the childish lilt of a simpleton:

"I thought you was the Devil, Mister, but you'm got no wings."

Smiley hesitated. If he moved forward, she might take fright again and run. He looked at her across the snow, trying to make her out. She seemed to be wearing a bonnet or shawl over her head, and a dark cape over her shoulders. In her hand she held a sprig of leaves, and these she gently waved back and forth as she spoke to him.

"But you'm carn't do nothin', Mister, 'cos I got the holly fer to hold yer. So you do bide there, Mister, for little Jane can hold yer." She shook the leaves vehemently towards him and began laughing softly. She still had one hand upon the door, and as she spoke her head lolled to one side.

"You bide away from little Jane, Mister, however pretty she'm do be."

"Yes, Jane," said Smiley softly, "you're a very pretty girl, I can see that; and that's a pretty cape you're wearing, Jane."

Evidently pleased with this, she clutched the lapels of her cape and turned slowly round, in a child's parody of a fine lady.

As she turned, Smiley saw the two empty sleeves of an overcoat swinging at her sides.

"There's some do laugh at Janie," she said, a note of petulance in her voice, "but there's not many seen the Devil fly, Mister. But Janie seed 'im, Janie seed 'im. Silver wings like fishes 'e done 'ad, Janie saw."

"Where did you find that coat, Janie?"

She put her hands together and shook her head slowly from side to side.

"He'm a bad one. Ooh, he'm a bad one, Mister," and she laughed softly. "I seed 'im flying, riding on the wind," she laughed again, "and the moon be'ind 'im, lightin' up the way! They'm close as sisters, moon and Devil."

On an impulse Smiley seized a handful of ivy from the side of the house and held it out to her, moving slowly forward as he did so.

"Do you like flowers, Janie? Here are flowers for Janie; pretty flowers for pretty Janie." He had nearly reached her when with remarkable speed she ran across the lawn, disappeared into the trees and ran off down the lane. Smiley let her go. He was drenched in sweat.

As soon as he reached the hotel he telephoned Detective Inspector Rigby.

VII

King Arthur's Church

The coffee lounge of the Sawley Arms resembles nothing so much as the Tropical Plants Pavilion at Kew Gardens. Built in an age when cactus was the most fashionable of plants and bamboo its indispensable companion, the lounge was conceived as the architectural image of a jungle clearing. Steel pillars, fashioned in segments like the trunk of a palm tree, supported a high glass roof whose regal dome replaced the African sky. Enormous urns of bronze or green-glazed earthenware contained all that was elegant and prolific in the cactus world, and between them very old residents could relax on sofas of spindly bamboo, sipping warm coffee and re-living the discomforts of safari.

Smiley's efforts to obtain a bottle of whisky and a syphon of soda at half past eleven at night were not immediately rewarded. It seemed that, like carrion from the carcass, the journalists had gone. The only sign of life in the hotel was the night porter, who treated his request with remote disapproval and advised him to go to bed. Smiley, by no means naturally persistent, discovered a half-crown in his overcoat pocket and thrust it a little irritably into the old man's hand. The result, though not magical, was effective, and by the time Rigby had made his way to the hotel, Smiley was seated in front of a bright gas fire in the coffee lounge with glasses and a whisky bottle before him.

Smiley retold his experiences of the evening with careful accuracy.

"It was the coat that caught my eye. It was a heavy overcoat like a man's," he concluded. "I remembered the blue belt and . . ." He left the sentence unfinished. Rigby nodded, got up and walked briskly across the lounge and through the swing doors to the porter's desk. Ten minutes later, he returned.

"I think we'd better go and pull her in," he said simply. "I've sent for a car."

"We?" asked Smiley.

"Yes, if you wouldn't mind. What's the matter? Are you frightened?"

"Yes," he replied. "Yes, I am."

The village of Pylle lies to the south of North Fields, upon a high spur which rises steeply from the flat, damp pastures of the Carne valley. It consists of a handful of stone cottages and a small inn where you may drink beer in the landlord's parlour. Seen from Carne playing fields, the village could easily be mistaken for an outcrop of rock upon a tor, for the hill on which it stands appears conical from the northern side. Local historians claim that Pylle is the oldest settlement in Dorset, that its name is Anglo-Saxon for harbour, and that it served the Romans as a port when all the lowlands around were covered by the sea. They will tell you, too, that King Arthur rested there after seven months at sea, and paid homage to Saint Andrew, the patron saint of sailors, on the site of Pylle Church, where he burned a candle for each month he had spent afloat; and that in the church, built to commemorate his visit and standing to this day lonely and untended on the hillside, there is a bronze coin as witness to his visit—the very one King Arthur gave to the verger before he set sail again for the Isle of Avalon.

Inspector William Rigby, himself a keen local historian, gave Smiley a somewhat terse précis of Pylle's legendary past as he drove cautiously along the snow-covered lanes.

"These small, out-of-the-way villages are pretty strange places," he concluded. "Often only three or four families, all so inbred you can no more sort them out than a barnful of cats. That's where your village idiots come from. They call it the Devil's Mark; I call it incest. They hate to have them in the village, you know—they'll drive them away at any price, like trying to wash away their shame, if you follow me."

"I follow you."

"This Jane's the religious sort. There's one or two of them turn that way. The villagers at Pylle are all Chapel now, see, so there's been no use for King Arthur's Church since Wesley. It's empty, falling to bits. There's a few from the valley go up to see it, for its history, like, but no one cares for it, or didn't not till Janie moved in."

"Moved in?"

"Yes. She's taken to cleaning the church out night and day, bringing in wild flowers and such. That's why they say she's a witch."

They passed Rode's house in silence and after turning a sharp bend began climbing the long steep hill that led to Pylle village. The snow in the lane was untouched and apart from occasional skidding they progressed without difficulty. The lower slopes of the hill were wooded, and the lane dark, until suddenly they emerged to find themselves on a smooth plateau, where a savage wind blew the fine snow like smoke across the fields, whipping it against the car. The snow had risen in drifts to one side of the lane, and the going became increasingly difficult.

Finally Rigby stopped the car and said:

"We'll walk from here, sir, if you don't mind."

"How far is it?"

"Short and sour, I'd say. That's the village straight ahead."

Through the windscreen, Smiley could discern behind the drifting veils of blown snow two low buildings about a quarter of a mile away. As he looked, a tall, muffled figure advanced towards them along the lane.

"That's Ted Mundy," said Rigby with satisfaction, "I told him to be here. He's the sergeant from Okeford." He leaned out of the car window and called merrily:

"Hullo, Ted there, you old buzzard, how be?" Rigby opened the back door of the car and the sergeant climbed in. Smiley and Mundy were briefly introduced.

"There's a light in the church," said Mundy, "but I don't know whether Janie's there. I can't ask no one in the village, see, or I'd have the whole lot round me. They thought she'd gone for good."

"Does she sleep there then, Ted? She got a bed there or something?" Rigby asked, and Smiley noticed with pleasure that his Dorset accent was more pronounced when he spoke to Mundy.

"So they say, Bill. I couldn't find no bed when I looked in there Saturday. But I tell you an odd thing, Bill. It seems Mrs. Rode used to come up here sometimes, to the chapel, to see Janie."

"I heard about that," said Rigby shortly. "Now which way's the church, Ted?"

"Over the hill," said Mundy. "Outside the village, in a paddock." He turned to Smiley. "That's quite common round here, sir, as I expect you know." Mundy spoke very slowly, choosing his words. "You see, when they had the plague they left their dead in the villages and moved away; not far though, on account of their land and the church. Terrible it was, terrible." Somehow Mundy managed to imply that the Black Death was a fairly recent disaster in those parts, if not actually within living memory.

They got out of the car, forcing the doors against the strong wind, and made their way towards the village, Mundy leading and Smiley in third place. The driven snow, fine and hard, stung their faces. It was an unearthly walk, high on that white hill on such a night. The curve of the bleak hill's crest and the moaning of the wind, the snow cloud which sped across the moon, the dismal, unlit cottages so cautiously passed, belonged to another corner of the world.

Mundy led them sharply to the left, and Smiley guessed that by avoiding the centre of the village he hoped to escape the notice of its inhabitants. After about twenty minutes' walking, often through deep snow, they found themselves following a low hedge between two fields. In the furthest corner of the right hand field they saw a pale light glimmering across the snow, so pale that at first Smiley had to look away from it, then run his eyes back along the line of that distant hedge to make sure he was not deceived. Rigby stopped, beckoning to the others.

"I'll take over now," he said. He turned to Smiley. "I'd be obliged, sir, if you'd stand off a little. If there's any trouble we don't want you mixed up in it, do we?"

"Of course."

"Ted Mundy, you come up by me."

They followed the hedge until they came to a stile. Through the gap in the hedge they saw the church clearly now, a low building more like a tithe barn than a church. At one end a pale glow, like the uncertain light of a candle, shone dimly through the leaded windows.

"She's there," said Mundy, under his breath, as he and Rigby moved forward, Smiley following some distance behind.

They were crossing the field now, Rigby leading, and the church drawing ever closer. New sounds disturbed the moaning of the storm; the parched creak of a door, the mutter of a crumbling roof, the incessant sigh of wind upon a dying house. The two men in front of Smiley had stopped, almost in the shadow of the church wall, and were whispering together. Then Mundy walked quietly away, disappearing round the corner of the church. Rigby waited a moment, then approached the narrow entrance in the rear wall, and pushed the door.

It opened slowly, creaking painfully on its hinges. Then he disappeared into the church. Smiley was waiting outside when suddenly above all the sounds of night he heard a scream, so taut and shrill and clear that it seemed to have no source, but to ride everywhere upon the wind, to mount the ravaged sky on wings; and Smiley had a vision of Mad Janie as he had seen her earlier that night, and he heard again in her demented cry the dreadful note of madness. For a moment he waited. The echo died. Then slowly, terrified, he walked through the snow to the open doorway.

Two candles and an oil lamp on the bare altar shed a dim light over the tiny chapel. In front of the altar, on the sanctuary step, sat Jane, looking vaguely towards them. Her vacuous face was daubed with stains of green and blue, her filthy clothes were threaded with sprigs of evergreen and all about her on the floor were the bodies of small animals and birds.

The pews were similarly decorated with dead creatures of all kinds; and on the altar, broken twigs and little heaps of holly leaves. Between the candles stood a crudely-fashioned cross. Stepping forward past Rigby, Smiley walked quickly down the aisle, past the lolling figure of Jane, until he stood before the altar. For a moment he hesitated, then turned and called softly to Rigby.

On the cross, draped over its three ends like a crude diadem, was a string of green beads.

VIII

Flowers For Stella

He woke with the echo of her scream in his ears. He had meant to sleep late, but his watch said half past seven. He put on his bedside lamp, for it was still half-dark, and peered owlishly round the room. There were his trousers, flung over the chair, the legs still sodden from the snow. There were his shoes; he'd have to buy another pair. And there beside him were the notes he had made early that morning before going to sleep, transcriptions from memory of some of Mad Jane's monologue on the journey back to Carne, a journey he would never forget. Mundy had sat with her in the back. She spoke to herself as a child does, asking questions and then in the patient tones of an adult for whom the reply is self-evident, providing the answer.

One obsession seemed to fill her mind: she had seen the devil. She had seen him flying on the wind, his silver wings stretched out behind him. Sometimes the recollection amused her, sometimes inflated her with a sense of her own importance or beauty, and sometimes it terrified her, so that she moaned and wept and begged him to go away. Then Mundy would speak kindly to her, and try to calm her. Smiley wondered whether policemen grew accustomed to the squalor of such things, to clothes that were no more than stinking rags wound round wretched limbs, to puling imbeciles

67

who clutched and screamed and wept. She must have been living on the run for nights on end, finding her food in the fields and dustbins since the night of the murder. . . . What had she done that night? What had she seen? Had she killed Stella Rode? Had she seen the murderer, and fancied *him* to be the devil flying on the wind? Why should she think that? If Janie did not kill Stella Rode, what had she seen that so frightened her that for three long winter nights she prowled in terror like an animal in the forest? Had the devil within taken hold of Janie and given power to her arm as she struck down Stella? Was that the devil who rode upon the wind?

But the beads and the coat and the footprints which were not hers—what of them? He lay there thinking, and achieving nothing. At last it was time to get up: it was the morning of the funeral.

As he was getting out of bed the telephone rang. It was Rigby. His voice sounded strained and urgent. "I want to se you," he said. "Can you call round?"

"Before or after the funeral?"

"Before, if possible. What about now?"

"I'll be there in ten minutes."

Rigby looked, for the first time since Smiley had met him, tired and worried.

"It's Mad Janie," he said. "The Chief thinks we should charge her."

"What for?"

"Murder," Rigby replied crisply, pushing a thin file across the table. "The old fool's made a statement . . . a sort of confession."

They sat in silence while Smiley read the extraordinary statement. It was signed with Mad Janie's mark—J. L.—drawn in a childish hand in letters an inch high. The constable who had taken it down had begun by trying to condense and simplify her account, but by the end of the first page he had obviously despaired. At last Smiley came to the description of the murder:

"*So I tells my darling, I tells her: 'You are a naughty creature to go with the devil,' but her did not hearken, see, and I took angry with her, but she paid no call. I can't abide them as go with devils in the night, and I told her. She ought to have had holly, mister, there's the truth. I told her, mister, but she never would hearken, and that's all Janie's saying, but she drove the devil off, Janie did, and there's one will thank me, that's my darling and I took her jewels for the saints I did, to pretty out the church, and a coat for to keep me warm.*"

Rigby watched him as he slowly replaced the statement on the desk.

"Well, what do you think of it?"

Smiley hesitated; "It's pretty good nonsense as it stands," he replied at last.

"Of course it is," said Rigby, with something like contempt. "She saw something, Lord knows what, when she was out on the prowl; stealing, I shouldn't wonder. She may have robbed the body, or else she picked up the beads where the murderer dropped them. We've traced the coat. Belonged to a Mr. Jardine, a baker in Carne East. Mrs. Jardine gave it to Stella Rode last Wednesday morning for the refugees. Janie must have pinched it from the conservatory. That's what she meant by 'a coat for to keep me warm.' But she no more killed Stella Rode than you or I did. What about the footprints, the glove-marks in the conservatory? Besides, she's not strong enough, Janie isn't, to heave that poor woman forty feet through the snow. This is a man's work, as anyone can see."

"Then what exactly . . . ?"

"We've called off the search, and I'm to prepare a case against one Jane Lyn of the village of Pylle for the wilful murder of Stella Rode. I wanted to tell you myself before you read it all over the papers. So that you'd know how it was."

"Thanks."

"In the meantime, if there's any help I can give

you, we're still willing." He hesitated, seemed about to say something, then to change his mind.

As he made his way down the wide staircase Smiley felt useless and very angry, which was scarcely the right frame of mind in which to attend a funeral.

It was an admirably conducted affair. Neither the flowers nor the congregation exceeded what was fitting to the occasion. She was not buried at the Abbey, out of deference perhaps to her simplicity of taste, but in the parish churchyard not far from North Fields. The Master was detained that day, as he was on most days, and had sent instead his wife, a small, very vague woman who had spent a long time in India. D'Arcy was much in evidence, fluttering here and there before the ceremony like an anxious beadle; and Mr. Cardew had come to guide poor Stella through the unfamiliarities of High Anglican procedure. The Hechts were there, Charles all in black, scrubbed and shining, and Shane in dramatic weeds, and a hat with a very broad brim.

Smiley, who, like the others, had arrived early in anticipation of the unwholesome public interest which the ceremony might arouse, found himself a seat near the entrance of the church. He watched each new arrival with interest, waiting for his first sight of Stanley Rode.

Several tradesmen arrived, pressed into bulging serge and black ties, and formed a small group south of the aisle, away from the staff and their wives. Soon they were joined by other members of the town community, women who had known Mrs. Rode at the Tabernacle; and then by Rigby, who looked straight at Smiley and gave no sign. Then on the stroke of three a tall old man walked slowly through the doorway, looking straight before him, neither knowing nor seeing anyone. Beside him was Stanley Rode.

It was a face which at first sight meant nothing to Smiley, seeming to have neither the imprint of temperament nor the components of character; it was a shallow, ordinary face, inclining to plumpness, and lacking quality. It matched his short, ordinary body and his black, ordinary hair; it was suitably compressed into an expression of sorrow. As Smiley watched him turn into the centre aisle and take his place among the principal mourners, it occurred to him that Rode's very walk and bearing successfully conveyed something entirely alien to Carne. If it is vulgar to wear a pen in the breast pocket of your jacket, to favour Fair Isle pullovers and brown ties, to bob a little and turn your feet out as you walk, then Rode beyond a shadow of doubt was vulgar, for though he did not now commit these sins, his manner implied them all.

They followed the coffin into the churchyard and gathered round the open grave. D'Arcy and Fielding were standing together, seemingly intent upon the service. The tall, elderly figure who had entered the church with Rode was now visibly moved, and Smiley guessed that he was Stella's father, Samuel Glaston. As the service ended, the old man walked quickly away from the crowd, nodding briefly to Rode, and disappeared into the church. He seemed to struggle as he went, like a man walking against a strong wind.

The little group moved slowly away from the graveside, until only Rode remained, an oddly stiff figure, taut and constrained, his eyes wide but somehow sightless, his mouth set in a strict, pedagogic line. Then, as Smiley watched, Rode seemed to wake from a dream; his body suddenly relaxed and he too walked slowly but quite confidently away from the grave towards the small group which by now had reassembled at the churchyard gate. As he did so, Fielding, at the edge of the group, caught sight of him approaching and, to Smiley's astonishment, walked deliberately and quite quickly away with an expression of strong distaste. It was not the calculated act of a man wishing to insult another, for it attracted the notice neither of Rode nor of anyone else standing by. Terence Fielding, for once, appeared to be in the grip of a genuine emotion, and indifferent to the impression he created.

Reluctantly Smiley approached the group. Rode was rather to one side, the D'Arcys were there, and three or four members of the staff. No one was talking much.

"Mr. Rode?" he enquired.

"That's right, yes." He spoke slowly, a trace of an accent carefully avoided.

"I'm representing Miss Brimley of the *Christian Voice*."

"Oh, yes."

"She was most anxious that the journal should be represented. I thought you would like to know that."

"I saw your wreath; very kind, I am sure."

"Your wife was one of our most loyal supporters," Smiley continued. "We regarded her almost as one of the family."

"Yes, she was very keen on the *Voice*." Smiley wondered whether Rode was always as impassive as this, or whether bereavement had made him listless.

"When did you come?" Rode asked suddenly.

"On Friday."

"Making a week-end of it, eh?"

Smiley was so astonished that for a moment he could think of nothing to say. Rode was still looking at him, waiting for an answer.

"I have one or two friends here . . . Mr. Fielding. . . ."

"Oh, Terence." Smiley was convinced that Rode was not on Christian-name terms with Fielding.

"I would like, if I may," Smiley ventured, "to write a small obituary for Miss Brimley. Would you have any objection?"

"Stella would have liked that."

"If you are not too upset, perhaps I could call round tomorrow for one or two details?"

"Certainly."

"Eleven o'clock?"

"It will be a pleasure," Rode replied, almost pertly, and they walked together to the churchyard gate.

IX

The Mourners

It was a cheap trick to play on a man who had suddenly
lost his wife. Smiley knew that. As he gently unlatched
the gate and entered the drive, where two nights ago he
had conducted his strange conversation with Jane Lyn,
he acknowledged that in calling on Rode under any pre-
text at such a time he was committing a thoroughly un-
principled act. It was a peculiarity of Smiley's character
that throughout the whole of his clandestine work he
had never managed to reconcile the means to the end.
A stringent critic of his own motives, he had discovered
after long observation that he tended to be less a creature of intellect than his tastes and habits might suggest;
once in the war he had been described by his superiors
as possessing the cunning of Satan and the conscience
of a virgin, which seemed to him not wholly unjust.

He pressed the bell and waited.

Stanley Rode opened the door. He was very neatly
dressed, very scrubbed.

"Oh hullo," he said, as if they were old friends. "I
say, you haven't got a car, have you?"

"I'm afraid I left it in London."

"Never mind." Rode sounded disappointed.
"Thought we might have gone out for a drive, had a
chat as we went. I get a bit fed-up, kicking around here
on my own. Miss D'Arcy asked me to stay over at their

place. Very good people they are, very good indeed; but
somehow I didn't wish it, not yet."

"I understand."

"Do you?" They were in the hall now, Smiley was
getting out of his overcoat, Rode waiting to receive it.
"I don't think many do—the loneliness I mean. Do you
know what they've done, the Master and Mr. D'Arcy?
They meant it well, I know. They've farmed out all my
correcting—my exam. correcting, you understand.
What am I supposed to do here, all on my own? I've no
teaching, nothing; they've all taken a hand. You'd think
they wanted to get rid of me."

Smiley nodded vaguely. They moved towards the
drawing-room, Rode leading the way.

"I know they did it for the best, as I said. But after
all, I've got to spend the time somehow. Simon Snow
got some of my division to correct. Have you met him
by any chance? Sixty-one per cent. He gave one boy—
sixty-one. The boy's an absolute fool; I told Fielding at
the beginning of the Half that he wouldn't possibly get
his Remove. Perkins his name is, a nice enough boy;
head of Fielding's house. He'd have been lucky to get
thirty per cent. . . . sixty-one, Snow gave him. I
haven't seen the papers yet, of course, but it's impossible,
quite impossible."

They sat down.

"Not that I don't want the boy to get on. He's a
nice enough boy, nothing special, but well-mannered.
Mrs. Rode and I meant to have him here to tea this
Half. We would have, in fact, if it hadn't been for . . ."
There was a moment's silence. Smiley was going to
speak when Rode stood up and said:

"I've a kettle on the stove, Mr. . . ."

"Smiley."

"I've a kettle on the stove, Mr. Smiley. May I
make you a cup of coffee?" That little stiff voice with
the corners carefully defined, like a hired morning suit,
thought Smiley.

Rode returned a few minutes later with a tray and
measured their coffee in precise quantities, according to
their taste.

Smiley found himself continually irritated by Rode's social assumptions, and his constant struggle to conceal his origin. You could tell all the time, from every word and gesture, what he was; from the angle of his elbow as he drank his coffee, from the swift, expert pluck at the knee of his trouser leg as he sat down.

"I wonder," Smiley began, "whether perhaps I might now . . ."

"Go ahead, Mr. Smiley."

"We are, of course, largely interested in Mrs. Rode's association with . . . our Church."

"Quite."

"You were married at Branxome, I believe."

"Branxome Hill Tabernacle; fine church." D'Arcy wouldn't have liked the way he said that; cocksure lad on a motor-bike. Pencils in the outside pocket.

"When was that?"

"September, fifty-one."

"Did Mrs. Rode engage in charitable work in Branxome? I know she was very active here."

"No, not at Branxome, but a lot here. She had to look after her father at Branxome, you see. It was refugee relief she was keen on here. That didn't get going much until late 1956—the Hungarians began it, and then this last year. . . ."

Smiley peered thoughtfully at Rode from behind his spectacles, forgot himself, blinked, and looked away.

"Did she take a large part in the social activities of Carne? Does the staff have its own Women's Institute and so on?" he asked innocently.

"She did a bit, yes. But, being Chapel, she kept mainly with the Chapel people from the town . . . you should ask Mr. Cardew about that; he's the Minister."

"But may I say, Mr. Rode, that she took an active part in school affairs as well?"

Rode hesitated.

"Yes, of course," he said.

"Thank you."

There was a moment's silence, then Smiley continued: "Our readers will, of course, remember Mrs. Rode as the winner of our Kitchen Hints competition. Was she a good cook, Mr. Rode?"

"Very good, for plain things, not fancy."

"Is there any little fact that you would specially like us to include, anything she herself would like to be remembered by?"

Rode looked at him with expressionless eyes. Then he shrugged.

"No, not really. I can't think of anything. Oh, you could say her father was a magistrate up North. She was proud of that."

Smiley finished his coffee and stood up.

"You've been very patient with me, Mr. Rode. We're most grateful, I assure you. I'll take care to send you an advance copy of our notice. . . ."

"Thanks. I did it for her, you see. She liked the *Voice*; always did. Grew up with it."

They shook hands.

"By the way, do you know where I can find old Mr. Glaston? Is he staying in Carne or has he returned to Branxome?"

"He was up here yesterday. He's going back to Branxome this afternoon. The police wanted to see him before he left."

"I see."

"He's staying at the Sawley."

"Thank you. I might try and see him before I go."

"When do you leave, then?"

"Quite soon, I expect. Goodbye, then, Mr. Rode. Incidentally——" Smiley began.

"Yes?"

"If ever you're in London and at a loose end, if ever you want a chat . . . and a cup of tea, we're always pleased to see you at the *Voice*, you know. Always."

"Thanks. Thanks very much Mr.——"

"Smiley."

"Thanks, that's very decent. No one's said that to me for a long time. I'll take you up on that one day. Very good of you."

"Goodbye." Again they shook hands; Rode's was dry and cool. Smooth.

He returned to the Sawley Arms, sat himself at a desk in the empty residents' lounge and wrote a note to Mr. Glaston:

> *Dear Mr. Glaston,*
> *I am here on behalf of Miss Brimley of the* Christian Voice. *I have some letters from Stella which I think you would like to see. Forgive me for bothering you at this sad moment; I understand you are leaving Carne this afternoon and wondered if I might see you before you left.*

He carefully sealed the envelope and took it to the reception desk. There was no one there, so he rang the bell and waited. At last a porter came, an old turnkey with a grey, bristly face, and after examining the envelope critically for a long time, he agreed, against an excessive fee, to convey it to Mr. Glaston's room. Smiley stayed at the desk, waiting for his answer.

Smiley himself was one of those solitaries who seem to have come into the world fully educated at the age of eighteen. Obscurity was his nature, as well as his profession. The byways of espionage are not populated by the brash and colourful adventurers of fiction. A man who, like Smiley, has lived and worked for years among his country's enemies learns only one prayer: that he may never, never be noticed. Assimilation is his highest aim, he learns to love the crowds who pass him in the street without a glance; he clings to them for his anonymity and his safety. His fear makes him servile— he could embrace the shoppers who jostle him in their impatience, and force him from the pavement. He could adore the officials, the police, the bus conductors, for the terse indifference of their attitudes.

But this fear, this servility, this dependence, had developed in Smiley a perception for the colour of human beings: a swift, feminine sensitivity to their characters and motives. He knew mankind as a huntsman

knows his cover, as a fox the wood. For a spy must
hunt while he is hunted, and the crowd is his estate. He
could collect their gestures and their words, record the
interplay of glance and movement, as a huntsman can
record the twisted bracken and the broken twig, or as a
fox detects the signs of danger.

Thus, while he waited patiently for Glaston's reply
and recalled the crowded events of the last forty-eight
hours, he was able to order and assess them with de-
tachment. What was the cause of D'Arcy's attitude to
Fielding, as if they were unwilling partners to a shabby
secret? Staring across the neglected hotel gardens towards Carne Abbey, he was able to glimpse behind the
lead roof of the Abbey the familiar battlements of the
school: keeping the new world out and the old world
secure. In his mind's eye he saw the Great Court now,
as the boys came out of Chapel: the black-coated
groups in the leisured attitudes of eighteenth-century
England. And he remembered the other school beside
the police station: Carne High School; a little tawdry
place like a porter's lodge in an empty graveyard, as
detached from the tones of Carne as its brick and flint
from the saffron battlements of School Hall.

Yes, he reflected, Stanley Rode had made a long,
long journey from the grammar school at Branxome.
And if he killed his wife, then the motive, Smiley was
sure, and even the means, were to be found in that hard
road to Carne.

"It was kind of you to come," said Glaston; "kind
of Miss Brimley to send you. They're good people at
the *Voice*; always were." He said this as if "good" were
an absolute quality with which he was familiar.

"You'd better read the letters, Mr. Glaston. The
second one will shock you, I'm afraid, but I'm sure
you'll agree that it would be wrong of me not to show it
to you." They were sitting in the lounge, the mammoth
plants like sentinels beside them.

He handed Glaston the two letters, and the old
man took them firmly and read them. He held them a
good way from him to read, thrusting his strong head

back, his eyes half closed, the crisp line of his mouth turned down at the corners. At last he said:

"You were with Miss Brimley in the war, were you?"

"I worked with John Landsbury, yes."

"I see. That's why she came to you?"

"Yes."

"Are you Chapel?"

"No."

He was silent for a while, his hands folded on his lap, the letters before him on the table.

"Stanley was Chapel when they married. Then he went over. Did you know that?"

"Yes."

"Where I come from in the North, we don't do that. Chapel was something we'd stood up for and won. Almost like the vote."

"I know."

His back was as straight as a soldier's. He looked stern rather than sad. Quite suddenly, his eyes turned towards Smiley, and he looked at him long and carefully.

"Are you a schoolmaster?" he asked, and it occurred to Smiley that in his day Samuel Glaston had been a very shrewd man of business.

"No. . . . I'm more or less retired."

"Married?"

"I was."

Again the old man fell silent, and Smiley wished he had left him alone.

"She was a great one for chatter," he said at last.

Smiley said nothing.

"Have you told the police?"

"Yes, but they knew already. That is, they knew that Stella thought her husband was going to murder her. She'd tried to tell Mr. Cardew. . . ."

"The Minister?"

"Yes. He thought she was overwrought and . . . deluded."

"Do you think she wasn't?"

"I don't know. I just don't know. But from what I

have heard of your daughter I don't believe she was un-balanced. *Something* roused her suspicions, something frightened her very much. I don't believe we can just disregard that. I don't believe it was a coincidence that she was frightened before she died. And therefore I don't believe that the beggar-woman murdered her."

Samuel Glaston nodded slowly. It seemed to Smiley that the old man was trying to show interest, partly to be polite, and partly because if he did not it would be a confession that he had lost interest in life itself.

Then, after a long silence, he carefully folded up the letters and gave them back. Smiley waited for him to speak, but he said nothing.

After a few moments Smiley got up and walked quietly from the room.

X

Little Women

Shane Hecht smiled, and drank some more sherry. "You must be dreadfully important," she said to Smiley, "for D'Arcy to serve decent sherry. What are you, *Almanach de Gotha?*"

"I'm afraid not. D'Arcy and I were both dining at Terence Fielding's on Saturday night and D'Arcy asked me for sherry."

"Terence is *wicked*, isn't he? Charles loathes him. I'm afraid they see Sparta in *quite* different ways. . . . Poor Terence. It's his last Half, you know."

"I know."

"So sweet of you to come to the funeral yesterday. I hate funerals, don't you? Black is so insanitary. I always remember King George V's funeral. Lord Sawley was at Court in those days, and gave Charles two tickets. So kind. I always think it's *spoilt* us for ordinary funerals in a way. Although I'm never quite *sure* about funerals, are you? I have a suspicion that they are largely a lower-class recreation; cherry brandy and seed cake in the parlour. I think the tendency of people like ourselves is for a *quiet* funeral these days; no flowers, just a short obituary and a memorial service later." Her small eyes were bright with pleasure. She finished her sherry and held out her empty glass to Smiley.

"Would you mind, dear. I hate sherry, but Felix is so mean."

Smiley filled her glass from the decanter on the table.

"Dreadful about the murder, wasn't it? That beggar-woman must be mad. Stella Rode was such a nice person, I always thought . . . and so *unusual*. She did such clever things with the same dress. . . . But she had such curious friends. All for Hans the woodcutter and Pedro the fisherman, if you know what I mean."

"Was she popular at Carne?"

Shane Hecht laughed gently: "No one is popular at Carne . . . but she wasn't easy to like. . . . She would wear black crêpe on Sundays. . . . Forgive me, but do the lower classes always do that? The townspeople liked her, I believe. They adore anyone who betrays Carne. But then she was a Christian Scientist or something."

"Baptist, I understand," said Smiley unthinkingly.

She looked at him for a moment with unfeigned curiosity. "How sweet," she murmured. "Tell me, what *are* you?"

Smiley made some facetious reply about being unemployed, and realised that it was only by a hair's-breadth that he had avoided explaining himself to Shane Hecht like a small boy. Her very ugliness, her size and voice, coupled with the sophisticated malice of her conversation, gave her the dangerous quality of command. Smiley was tempted to compare her with Fielding, but for Fielding other people scarcely existed. For Shane Hecht they did exist: they were there to be found wanting in the minute tests of social behaviour, to be ridiculed, cut off and destroyed.

"I read in the paper that her father was quite well off. From the North. Second generation. Remarkable really how *unspoilt* she was . . . so natural. . . . You wouldn't think she *needed* to go to the launderette or to make friends with beggars. . . . Though, of course, the Midlands are different, aren't they? Only about three good families between Ipswich and Newcastle. Where did you say you came from, dear?"

"London."

"How nice. I went to tea with Stella once. Milk in first and Indian. So different," and she looked at Smiley suddenly and said "I'll tell you something. She almost aroused an admiration in me, I found her so insufferable. She was one of those tiresome little snobs who think that only the humble are virtuous." Then she smiled and added, "I even agreed with Charles about Stella Rode, and that's saying something. If you're a student of mankind, do go and have a look at him, the contrast is riveting." But at that moment they were joined by D'Arcy's sister, a bony, virile woman with untidy grey hair and an arrogant, hunting mouth.

"Dorothy darling," Shane murmured; "such a lovely party. So *kind*. And so *exciting* to meet somebody from London, don't you think? We were talking about poor Mrs. Rode's funeral."

"Stella Rode may have been damn' bad form, Shane, but she did a lot for my refugees."

"Refugees?" asked Smiley innocently.

"Hungarians. Collecting for them. Clothes, furniture, money. One of the few wives who *did* anything." She looked sharply at Shane Hecht, who was smiling benignly past her towards her husband: "Busy little creature, she was; didn't mind rolling her sleeves up, going from door to door. Got her little women on to it at the Baptist chapel and brought in a mass of stuff. You've got to hand it to them, you know. They've got *spirit*. Felix, more sherry!"

There were about twenty in the two rooms, but Smiley, who had arrived a little late, found himself attached to a group of about eight who stood nearest the door: D'Arcy and his sister; Charles and Shane Hecht; a young mathematician called Snow and his wife; a curate from the Abbey and Smiley himself, bewildered and mole-like behind his spectacles. Smiley looked quickly round the room, but could see no sign of Fielding.

". . . Yes," Dorothy D'Arcy continued, "she was a good little worker, very . . . right to the end. I went over there on Friday with that parson man from the tin tabernacle—Cardew—to see if there was any refugee stuff to tidy up. There wasn't a thing out of place—every bit of clothing she had was all packed up and addressed; we just had to send it off. She was a damn' good little worker, I will say. Did a splendid job at the bazaar, you know."

"Yes, darling," said Shane Hecht sweetly. "I remember it well. It was the day I presented her to lady Sawley. She wore such a *nice* little hat—the one she wore on Sundays, you know. And *so* respectful. She called her 'my lady'." She turned to Smiley and breathed: "Rather feudal, don't you think, dear? I always like that: so few of us left."

The mathematician and his wife were talking to Charles Hecht in a corner and a few minutes later Smiley managed to extricate himself from the group and join them.

Ann Snow was a pretty girl with a rather square face and a turned-up nose. Her husband was tall and thin, with an agreeable stoop. He held his sherry glass between straight, slender fingers as if it were a chemical retort and when he spoke he seemed to address the sherry rather than his listener; Smiley remembered them from the funeral. Hecht was looking pink and rather cross, sucking at his pipe. They talked in a desultory way, their conversation dwarfed by the exchanges of the adjoining group. Hecht eventually drifted away from them, still frowning and withdrawn, and stood ostentatiously alone near the door.

"Poor Stella," said Ann Snow after a moment's silence. "Sorry," she added. "I can't get her out of my mind yet. It seems mad, just mad. I mean why should she *do* it, that Janie woman?"

"Did you like Stella?" Smiley asked.

"Of course we did. She was sweet. We've been here four Halves now, but she was the only person here who's ever been *kind* to us." Her husband said nothing, just nodded at his sherry. "Simon wasn't a boy at Carne, you see—most of the staff were—so we didn't know anyone and no one was really interested. They all pretended to be terribly pleased with us, of course, but it was Stella who really . . ."

Dorothy D'Arcy was descending on them. "Mrs. Snow," she said crisply, "I've been meaning to talk to you. I want you to take over Stella Rode's job on the refugees." She cast an appraising look in Simon's direction: "The Master's very keen on refugees."

"Oh, my goodness!" Ann Snow replied, aghast. "I couldn't possibly, Miss D'Arcy, I . . ."

"Couldn't? Why couldn't you? You helped Mrs. Rode with her stall at the bazaar, didn't you?"

"So that's where she got her clothes from," breathed Shane Hecht behind them. Ann was fumbling on:

"But . . . well I haven't quite got Stella's nerve, if you understand what I mean; and besides, she was a Baptist: all the locals helped her and gave her things, and they all liked her. With me it would be different."

"Lot of damn' nonsense," declared Miss D'Arcy, who spoke to all her juniors as if they were grooms or erring children; and Shane Hecht beside her said: "Baptists are the people who don't like private pews, aren't they? I do so agree—one feels that if one's paid one simply has to go."

The curate who had been talking cricket in a corner, was startled into mild protest: "Oh, come, Mrs. Hecht, the private pew had many advantages . . ." and embarked on a diffuse apologia for ancient custom, to which Shane listened with every sign of the most assiduous interest. When at last he finished she said: "Thank you, William dear, so sweet," turned her back on him and added to Smiley in a stage whisper: "William Trumper—one of Charles' old pupils—such a triumph when he passed his Certificate."

Smiley, anxious to dissociate himself from Shane Hecht's vengeance on the curate, turned to Ann Snow, but she was still at the mercy of Miss D'Arcy's charitable intentions, and Shane was still talking to him:

"The only Smiley I ever heard of married Lady Ann Sercombe at the end of the war. She left him soon afterwards, of course. A very curious match. I understand he was quite unsuitable. She was Lord Sawley's cousin, you know. The Sawleys have been connected with Carne for four hundred years. The present heir is a pupil of Charles; we often dine at the Castle. I never did hear what became of Ann Sercombe . . . she went to Africa, you know . . . or was it India? No it was America. So tragic. One doesn't talk about it at the Castle." For a moment the noise in the room stopped. For a moment, no more, he could discern nothing but the steady gaze of Shane Hecht upon him, and knew she was waiting for an answer. And then she released him as if to say: "I could crush you, you see. But I won't, I'll let you live," and she turned and walked away.

He contrived to take his leave at the same time as Ann and Simon Snow. They had an old car and insisted on running Smiley back to his hotel. On the way there, he said:

"If you have nothing better to do, I would be happy to give you both dinner at my hotel. I imagine the food is dreadful."

The Snows protested and accepted, and a quarter of an hour later they were all three seated in a corner of the enormous dining-room of the Sawley Arms, to the great despondency of three waiters and a dozen generations of Lord Sawley's forbears, puffy men in crumbling pigment.

"We really got to know her our second Half," Ann Snow ran on. "Stella didn't do much mixing with the other wives—she'd learnt her lesson by then. She didn't go to coffee parties and things, so it was really luck that we did meet. When we first came there wasn't a staff house available for us: we had to spend the first Half in a hotel. We moved in to a little house in Bread Street at the end of our second Half. Moving was chaos—Simon was examining for the scholarships and we were terribly broke, so we had to do everything we possibly could for ourselves. It was a wet Thursday morning when we moved. The rain was simply teeming down; but none of our good pieces would get in through the front door, and in the end Mulligan's just dumped me on the doorstep and let me sort it out." She laughed, and Smiley thought what an agreeable child she was. "They were

absolutely foul. They would have just driven off, I
think, but they wanted a cheque as soon as they'd done
the delivery, and the bill was pounds more than the esti-
mate. I hadn't got the cheque-book, of course. Simon
had gone off with it. Mulligan's even threatened to take
all the stuff away again. It was monstrous. I think I was
nearly in tears." She nearly is now, thought Smiley.
"Then out of the blue Stella turned up. I can't think
how she even knew we were moving—I'm sure no one
else did. She'd brought an overall and an old pair of
shoes and she'd come to help. When she saw what was
going on she didn't bother with the men at all, just went
to a phone and rang Mr. Mulligan himself. I don't
know what she said to him, but she made the foreman
talk to him afterwards and there was no more trouble
after that. She was terribly happy—happy to *help*. She
was that sort of person. They took the door right out
and managed to get everything in. She was marvellous
at helping without managing. The rest of the wives," she
added bitterly, "are awfully good at managing, but don't
help at all."

Smiley nodded, and discreetly filled their glasses.

"Simon's leaving," Ann said, suddenly confiden-
tial. "He's got a grant and we're going back to Oxford.
He's going to do a D.Phil. and get a University job."

They drank to his success, and the conversation
turned to other things until Smiley asked: "What's
Rode himself like to work with?"

"He's a good schoolmaster," said Simon, slowly,
"but tiring as a colleague."

"Oh, he was *quite* different from Stella," said Ann.
"Terribly Carne-minded. D'Arcy adopted him and he
got the bug. Simon says all the grammar school people
go that way—it's the fury of the convert. It's sickening.
He even changed his religion when he got to Carne.
Stella didn't, though; she wouldn't dream of it."

"The Established Church has much to offer at
Carne," Simon observed, and Smiley enjoyed the dry
precision of his delivery.

"Stella can't exactly have hit it off with Shane
Hecht," Smiley probed gently.

"Of *course* she didn't!" Ann declared angrily. "Shane was horrid to her, always sneering at her because she was honest and simple about the things she liked. Shane hated Stella—I think it was because Stella didn't *want* to be a lady of quality. She was quite happy to be herself. That's what really worried Shane. Shane likes people to compete so that she can make fools of them."

"So does Carne," said Simon, quietly.

"She was awfully good at helping out with the refugees. That was how she got into real trouble." Ann Snow's slim hands gently rocked her brandy glass.

"Trouble?"

"Just before she died. Hasn't anyone told you? About her frightful row with D'Arcy's sister?"

"No."

"Of course, they wouldn't have done. Stella never gossiped."

"Let me tell you," said Simon. "It's a good story. When the Refugee Year business started, Dorothy D'Arcy was fired with charitable enthusiasm. So was the Master. Dorothy's enthusiasms always seem to correspond with his. She started collecting clothes and money and packing them off to London. All very laudable, but there was a perfectly good town appeal going, launched by the Mayor. That wasn't good enough for Dorothy, though: the school must have its own appeal; you can't mix your charity. I think Felix was largely behind it. Anyway, after the thing had been going for a few months the refugee centre in London apparently wrote to Dorothy and asked whether anyone would be prepared to accommodate a refugee couple. Instead of publicising the letter, Dorothy wrote straight back and said she would put them up herself. So far so good. The couple turned up, Dorothy and Felix pointed a proud finger at them and the local press wrote it all up as an example of British humanity.

"About six weeks later, one afternoon, these two turned up on Stella's doorstep. The Rodes and the D'Arcys are neighbours, you see, and anyway Stella had tried to take an interest in Dorothy's refugees. The woman was in floods of tears and the husband was shouting blue murder, but that didn't worry Stella. She had them straight into the drawing-room and gave them a cup of tea. Finally, they managed to explain in basic English that they had run away from the D'Arcy's because of the treatment they received. The girl was expected to work from morning till night in the kitchen, and the husband was acting as unpaid kennel-boy for those beastly spaniels that Dorothy breeds. The ones without noses."

"King Charles," Ann prompted.

"It was about as awful as it could be. The girl was pregnant and he was a fully qualified engineer, so neither of them were exactly suited to domestic service. They told Stella that Dorothy was away till the evening—she'd gone to a dog show. Stella advised them to stay with her for the time being, and that evening she went round and told Dorothy what had happened. She had quite a nerve, you see. Although it wasn't nerve really. She just did the simple thing. Dorothy was furious, and demanded that Stella should return 'her refugees' immediately. Stella replied that she was sure that they wouldn't come, and went home. When Stella got home she rang up the refugee people in London and asked their advice. They sent a woman down to see Dorothy and the couple, and the result was that they returned to London the following day. . . . You can imagine what Shane Hecht would have made of that story."

"Didn't she ever find out?"

"Stella never told anyone except us, and we didn't pass it on. Dorothy just let it be known that the refugees had gone to some job in London, and that was that."

"How long ago did this happen?"

"They left exactly three weeks ago," said Ann to her husband. "Stella told me about it when she came to supper the night you were in Oxford for your interview. That was three weeks ago tonight." She turned to Smiley:

"Poor Simon's been having an awful time. Felix

D'Arcy unloaded all Rode's exam. correcting on to him. It's bad enough doing one person's correction—two is frantic."

"Yes," replied Simon reflectively. "It's been a bad week. And rather humiliating in a way. Several of the boys who were up to me for science last Half are now in Rode's forms. I'd regarded one or two of them as practically unteachable, but Rode seems to have brought them on marvellously. I corrected one boy's paper—Perkins—sixty-one per cent for elementary science. Last Half he got fifteen per cent in a much easier paper. He only got his Remove because Fielding raised hell. He was in Fielding's house."

"Oh I know—a red-haired boy, a prefect."

"Good Lord," cried Simon. "Don't say you know him?"

"Oh, Fielding introduced us," said Smiley vaguely. "Incidentally—no one else ever mentioned that incident to you about Miss D'Arcy's refugees, did they? Confirmed it, as it were?"

Ann Snow looked at him oddly. "No. Stella told us about it, but of course Dorothy D'Arcy never referred to it at all. She must have *hated* Stella, though."

He saw them to their car, and waited despite their protests while Simon cranked it. At last they drove off, the car bellowing down the silent street. Smiley stood for a moment on the pavement, an odd, lonely figure peering down the empty road.

XI

A Coat To Keep Her Warm

A dog that had not bitten the postman; a devil that rode upon the wind; a woman who knew that she would die; a little, worried man in an overcoat standing in the snow outside his hotel and the laborious chime of the Abbey clock telling him to go to bed.

Smiley hesitated, then with a shrug crossed to the hotel entrance, mounted the step and entered the cheap, yellow light of the residents' hall. He walked slowly up the stairs.

He detested the Sawley Arms. That muted light in the hall was typical: inefficient, antiquated and smug. Like the waiters in the dining-room and the lowered voices in the residents' lounge, like his own hateful bedroom with its blue and gilt urns, and the framed tapestry of a Buckinghamshire garden.

His room was bitterly cold; the maid must have opened the window. He put a shilling in the meter and lit the gas. The fire bubbled grumpily and went out. Muttering, Smiley looked around for some paper to write on, and discovered some, much to his surprise, in the drawer of the writing desk. He changed into his pyjamas and dressing gown and crawled miserably into bed. After sitting there uncomfortably for some minutes he got up, fetched his overcoat and spread it over the eiderdown. A coat for to keep her warm. . . .

How did her statement read? "There's one will thank me, that's my darling and I took her jewels for the saints I did, and a coat for to keep me warm. . . ." The coat had been given to Stella last Wednesday for the refugees. It seemed reasonable to assume from the way the statement read that Janie had taken the coat from the outhouse at the same time as she took the beads from Stella's body. But Dorothy D'Arcy had been round there on Friday morning—of course she had, with Mr. Cardew—she was talking about it at her party that very evening: "There wasn't a thing out of place— every bit of clothing she had was all packed up and ad- dressed—a damn' good little worker, I will say. . . ." Then why hadn't Stella packed the overcoat? If she packed everything else, why not the overcoat too?

Or had Janie stolen the coat earlier in the day, be- fore Stella made her parcel? If that was so, it went some way to weakening the case against her. But it was not so. It was not so because it was utterly improbable that Janie should steal a coat in the afternoon and return to the house the same evening.

"Start at the beginning," Smiley muttered, a little sententiously to the crested paper on his lap. "Janie stole the coat at the same time as she stole the beads— that is, after Stella was dead. Therefore either the coat was not packed with the other clothes, or . . ."

Or what? *Or somebody else, somebody who was not Stella Rode, packed up the clothes after Stella had died and before Dorothy D'Arcy and Mr. Cardew went round to North Fields on Friday morning. And why the devil, thought Smiley, should anyone do that?*

It had been one of Smiley's cardinal principles in research, whether among the incunabula of an obscure poet or the laboriously gathered fragments of intelli- gence, not to proceed beyond the evidence. A fact, once logically arrived at, should not be extended beyond its natural significance. Accordingly he did not speculate with the remarkable discovery he had made, but turned his mind to the most obscure problem of all: motive for murder.

He began writing:

"Dorothy D'Arcy—resentment after refugee fiasco. As a motive for murder—definitely thin." Yet why did she seem to go out of her way to sing Stella's praises?

"Felix D'Arcy—resented Stella Rode for not observing Carne's standards. As a motive for murder—ludicrous.

"Shane Hecht—hatred.

"Terence Fielding—in a sane world, no conceivable motive."

Yet was it a sane world? Year in year out they must share the same life, say the same things to the same people, sing the same hymns. They had no money, no hope. The world changed, fashion changed; the women saw it second-hand in the glossy papers, took in their dresses and pinned up their hair, and hated their husbands a little more. Shane Hecht—did she kill Stella Rode? Did she conceal in the sterile omniscience of her huge body not only hatred and jealousy, but the courage to kill? Was she frightened for her stupid husband, frightened of Rode's promotion, of his cleverness? Was she really so angry when Stella refused to take part in the rat race of gentility?

Rigby was right—it was impossible to know. You had to be ill, you had to be sick to understand, you had to be there in the sanatorium, not for weeks, but for years, had to be one in the line of white beds, to know the smell of their food and the greed in their eyes. You had to hear it and see it, to be part of it, to know their rules and recognise their transgressions. This world was compressed into a mould of anomalous conventions: blind, pharasaical but real.

Yet some things were written plain enough; the curious bond which tied Felix D'Arcy and Terence Fielding despite their mutual dislike; D'Arcy's reluctance to discuss the night of the murder; Fielding's evident preference for Stella Rode rather than her husband; Shane Hecht's contempt for everyone.

He could not get Shane out of his mind. If Carne were a rational place, and somebody had to die, then

Shane Hecht should clearly be the one. She was a depository of other people's secrets, she had an infallible sense for weakness. Had she not found even Smiley out? She had taunted him with his wretched marriage, she had played with him for her own pleasure. Yes, she was an admirable candidate for murder.

But why on earth should Stella die? Why and how? Who tied up the parcel after her death? And why?

He tried to sleep, but could not. Finally, as the Abbey clock chimed three, he put the light on again and sat up. The room was much warmer and at first Smiley wondered if someone had switched on the central heating in the middle of the night, after it had been off all day. Then he became aware of the sound of rain outside; he went to the window and parted the curtains. A steady rain was falling; by tomorrow the snow would be washed away. Two policemen walked slowly down the road; he could hear the squelch of their boots as they trod in the melting snow. Their wet capes glistened in the arc of the street lamp.

And suddenly he seemed to hear Rigby's voice: "Blood everywhere. Whoever killed her must have been covered in it." And then Mad Janie calling to him across the moonlit snow: "Janie seed 'im . . . silver wings like fishes . . . flying on the wind . . . there's not many seen the devil fly. . . ." Of course: the parcel! He remained a long time at the window, watching the rain. Finally, content at last, he climbed back into bed and fell asleep.

He tried to telephone Miss Brimley throughout the morning. Each time she was out and he left no message. Eventually, at about midday, he spoke to her:

"George, I'm terribly sorry—some missionary is in London—I had to go for an interview and I've got a Baptist Conference this afternoon. They've both got to be in this week. Will first thing tomorrow do?"

"Yes," said Smiley. "I'm sure it will." There was no particular hurry. There were one or two ends he wanted to tie up that afternoon, anyway.

XII

Uncomfortable Words

He enjoyed the bus. The conductor was a very surly man with a great deal to say about the bus company, and why it lost money. Gently encouraged by Smiley, he expanded wonderfully so that by the time they arrived at Sturminster he had transformed the Directors of the Dorset and General Traction Company into a herd of Gadarene swine charging into the abyss of voluntary bankruptcy. The conductor directed Smiley to the Sturminster kennels, and when he alighted in the tiny village he set out confidently towards a group of cottages which stood about a quarter of a mile beyond the church, on the Okeford road.

He had a nasty feeling he wasn't going to like Mr. Harriman. The very fact that D'Arcy had described him as a superior type of person inclined Smiley against him. Smiley was not opposed to social distinctions but he liked to make his own.

A notice stood at the gate: *"Sturminster Kennels, proprietor, C. F. Reid-Harriman, Veterinary Surgeon. Breeder of Alsatian and Labrador Dogs. Boarding."*

A narrow path led to what seemed to be a backyard. There was washing everywhere, shirts, underclothes and sheets, most of it khaki. There was a rich smell of dog. There was a rusted hand-pump with a dozen or so dog leads draped over it, and there was a small girl. She watched him sadly as he picked his way through the thick mud towards the door. He pulled on the bell-rope and waited. He tried again, and the child said:

"It doesn't work. It's bust. It's been bust for years."

"Is anyone at home?" Smiley asked.

"I'll see," she replied coolly, and after another long look at him she walked round the side of the house and disappeared from view. Then Smiley heard from inside the house the sound of someone approaching, and a moment later the door opened.

"Good day to you." He had sandy hair and a moustache. He wore a khaki shirt and a khaki tie of a lighter shade; old Service dress trousers and a tweed jacket with leather buttons.

"Mr. Harriman?"

"Major," he replied lightly. "Not that it matters, old boy. What can we do for you?"

"I'm thinking of buying an Alsatian," Smiley replied, "as a guard dog."

"Surely. Come in, won't you. Lady wife's out. Ignore the child: she's from next door. Just hangs around; likes the dogs." He followed Harriman into the living room and they sat down. There was no fire.

"Where are you from?" Harriman asked.

"I'm staying at Carne at the moment; my father lives over at Dorchester. He's getting on and he's nervous, and he wants me to find him a good dog. There's a gardener to look after it in the daytime, feed it and exercise it and so on. The gardener doesn't live in at night, of course, and it's at night that the old man gets so worried. I've been meaning to get him a dog for some time—this recent business at Carne rather brought it home to me." Harriman ignored the hint.

"Gardener good chap?"

"Yes, very."

"You don't want anything brilliant," said Harriman. "You want a good, steady type. I'd take a bitch if I were you." His hands were dark brown, his wrists too. His handkerchief was tucked into his cuff. Smiley noticed that his wrist-watch faced inwards, conforming with the obscure rites of the military *demimonde* from which he seemed to come.

"What will it do, a dog like that? Will it attack, or what?"

"Depends how she's trained, old boy; depends how she's trained. She'll warn, though; that's the main thing. Frighten the fellers away. Shove a notice up, 'Fierce Dog,' let her sniff at the tradesmen a bit and the word will get around. You won't get a burglar within a mile of the place."

They walked out into the garden again, and Harriman led the way to an enclosure with half a dozen Alsatian puppies yapping furiously at them through the wire.

"They're good little beasts, all of them," he shouted. "Game as hell." He unlocked the door and finally emerged with a plump bitch puppy chewing fiercely at his jacket.

"This little lady might do you," he said. "We can't show her—she's too dark."

Smiley pretended to hesitate, allowed Harriman to persuade him and finally agreed. They went back into the house.

"I'd like to pay a deposit," said Smiley, "and collect her in about ten days. Would that be all right?" He gave Harriman a cheque for five pounds and again they sat down, Harriman foraging in his desk for inoculation certificates and pedigrees. Then Smiley said:

"It's a pity Mrs. Rode didn't have a dog, isn't it? I mean, it might have saved her life."

"Oh, she *had* a dog, but she had it put down just before she was killed," said Harriman. "Damned odd story between ourselves. She was devoted to the beast. Odd little mongrel, bit of everything, but she loved it. Brought it here one day with some tale about it biting the postman, got me to put it down—said it was dangerous. It wasn't anything of the sort. Some friends of mine in Carne made enquiries. No complaints anywhere. Postman liked the brute. Damned silly sort of lie to tell in a small community. Bound to be found out."

"Why on earth did she tell it then?"

Harriman made a gesture which particularly irritated Smiley. He ran his forefinger down the length of his nose, then flicked either side of his absurd moustache very quickly. There was something shamefaced about the whole movement, as if he were assuming the ways of senior officers, and fearful of rebuke.

"She was trouble," he said crisply. "I can spot 'em. I've had a few in the regiment, wives who are trouble. Little simpering types. Butter-wouldn't-melt, holier-than-thou. Arrange the flowers in the church and all that—pious as you please. I'd say she was the hysterical kind, self-dramatising, weeping all over the house for days on end. Anything for a bit of drama."

"Was she popular?" Smiley offered him a cigarette.

"Shouldn't think so. Thanks. She wore black on Sundays, I gather. Typical. We used to call them 'crows' out East, the ones who wore black—Sunday virgins. They were O.D. mostly—other denominations. Not C. of E.—some were Romans, mind. . . . I hope I'm not . . ."

"Not at all."

"You never know, do you? Can't stand 'em myself; no prejudice, but I don't like Romans—that's what my old father used to say."

"Did you know her husband?"

"Not so well, poor devil, not so well."

Harriman, Smiley reflected, seemed to have a great deal more sympathy for the living than the dead. Perhaps soldiers were like that. He wouldn't know.

"He's terribly cut up, I hear. Dreadful shock—fortunes of war, eh?" he added and Smiley nodded. "He's the other type. Humble origin, good officer qualities, credit to the mess. Those are the ones that cut up most, the ones women get at."

They walked along the path to the gate. Smiley said goodbye, and promised to return in a week or so to collect the puppy. As he walked away Harriman called to him:

"Oh—incidentally . . ."

Smiley stopped and turned round.

"I'll pay that cheque in, shall I, and credit you with the amount?"

"Of course," said Smiley. "That will do very well," and he made his way to the bus stop pondering on the strange byways of the military mind.

The same bus took him back to Carne, the same conductor railed against his employers, the same driver drove the entire distance in second gear. He got out at the station and made his way to the red-brick Tabernacle. Gently opening the Gothic door, made of thickly-varnished ochre pine, he stepped inside. An elderly woman in an apron was polishing the heavy brass chandelier which hung over the centre aisle. He waited a moment, then tiptoed up to her and asked for the Minister. She pointed towards the vestry door. Obeying her mimed directions, he crossed to it, knocked and waited. A tall man in a clerical collar opened the door.

"I'm from the *Christian Voice*," said Smiley quietly. "Can I have a word with you?"

Mr. Cardew led him through the side entrance and into a small vegetable garden, carefully tilled, with bright yellow paths running between the empty beds. The sun shone through the crisp air. It was a cold, beautiful day. They crossed the garden and entered a paddock. The ground was hard despite last night's rain, and the grass short. They strolled side by side, talking as they went.

"This is Lammas Land, belonging to the School. We hold our fêtes here in the summer. It's very practical."

Cardew seemed a little out of character. Smiley, who had a rather childish distrust of clergymen, had expected a Wesleyan hammer, a wordy, forbidding man with a taste for imagery.

"Miss Brimley, our editor, sent me," Smiley began. "Mrs. Rode subscribed to our journal; her family has taken it since it began. She was almost a part of the family. We wanted to write an obituary about her work for the Church."

"I see."

"I managed to have a word with her husband; we wanted to be sure to strike the right note."

"What did he say?"

"He said I should speak to you about her work—her refugee work particularly."

They walked on in silence for a while, then Cardew said, "She came from up North, near Derby. Her father used to be a man of substance in the North—though money never altered him."

"I know."

"I've known the family for years, off and on. I saw her old father before the funeral."

"What may I say about her work for the Church, her influence on the Chapel community here? May I say she was universally loved?"

"I'm afraid," said Cardew, after a slight pause, "that I don't hold much with that kind of writing, Mr. Smiley. People are never universally loved, even when they're dead." His North Country accent was strong.

"Then what may I say?" Smiley persisted.

"I don't know," Cardew replied evenly. "And when I don't know, I usually keep quiet. But since you're good enough to ask me, I've never met an angel, and Stella Rode was no exception."

"But was she not a leading figure in refugee work?"

"Yes. Yes, she was."

"And did she not encourage others to make similar efforts?"

"Of course. She was a good worker."

They walked on together in silence. The path across the field led downwards, then turned and followed a stream which was almost hidden by the tangled gorse and hawthorn on either side. Beyond the stream was a row of stark elm trees, and behind them the familiar outline of Carne.

"Is that all you wanted to ask me?" said Cardew suddenly.

"No," replied Smiley. "Our editor was very worried by a letter she received from Mrs. Rode just before her death. It was a kind of . . . accusation. We put the

matter before the police. Miss Brimley reproaches herself in some way for not having been able to help her.
It's illogical, perhaps, but there it is. I would like to be
able to assure her that there was no connection between
Stella Rode's death and this letter. That is another reason for my visit. . . ."

"Whom did the letter accuse?"

"Her husband."

"I should tell your Miss Brimley," said Cardew
slowly, and with some emphasis, "that she has nothing
whatever for which to reproach herself."

XIII

The Journey Home

It was Monday evening. At about the time that Smiley returned to his hotel after his interview with Mr. Cardew, Tim Perkins, the Head of Fielding's house, was taking his leave of Mrs. Harlowe, who taught him the 'cello. She was a kindly woman, if neurotic, and it distressed her to see him so worried. He was quite the best pupil that Carne had sent her, and she liked him.

"You played foully today, Tim," she said as she wished him goodbye at the door, "quite foully. You needn't tell me—you've only got one more Half and you still haven't got three passes in A Level and you've got to get your remove, and you're in a tizz. We won't practise next Monday if you don't want—just come and have buns and we'll play some records."

"Yes, Mrs. Harlowe." He strapped his music-case on to the carrier of his bicycle.

"Lights working, Tim?"

"Yes, Mrs. Harlowe."

"Well, don't try and beat the record tonight, Tim. You've plenty of time till Boys' Tea. Remember the lane's still quite slippery from the snow."

Perkins said nothing. He pushed the bicycle on to the gravel path and started towards the gate.

"Haven't you forgotten something, Tim?"

"Sorry, Mrs. Harlowe."

He turned back and shook hands with her in the doorway. She always insisted on that.

"Look, Tim, what *is* the matter? Have you done something silly? You can tell me, can't you? I'm not Staff, you know."

Perkins hesitated, then said:

"It's just exams., Mrs. Harlowe."

"Are your parents all right? No trouble at home?"

"No, Mrs. Harlowe; they're fine." Again he hesitated, then: "Good night, Mrs. Harlowe."

"Good night."

She watched him close the gate behind him and cycle off down the narrow lane. He would be in Carne in quarter of an hour; it was downhill practically all the way.

Usually he loved the ride home. It was the best moment of the week. But tonight he hardly noticed it. He rode fast, as he always did; the hedge raced against the dark sky and the rabbits scuttled from the beam of his lamp, but tonight he hardly noticed them.

He would have to tell somebody. He should have told Mrs. Harlowe; he wished he had. She'd know what to do. Mr. Snow would have been all right, but he wasn't up to him for science any longer, he was up to Rode. That was half the trouble. That and Fielding.

He could tell True—yes, that's who he'd tell, he'd tell True. He'd go to Miss Truebody tonight after evening surgery and he'd tell her the truth. His father would never get over it, of course, because it meant failure and perhaps disgrace. It meant not getting to Sandhurst at the end of next Half, it meant more money they couldn't afford. . . .

He was coming to the steepest part of the hill. The hedge stopped on one side and instead there was a marvellous view of Sawley Castle against the night sky, like a backcloth for *Macbeth*. He loved acting—he wished the Master let them act at Carne.

He leant forward over the handlebars and allowed himself to gather speed to go through the shallow ford at the bottom of the hill. The cold air bit into his face, and for a moment he almost forgot. . . . Suddenly he braked; felt the bike skid wildly beneath him.

Something was wrong; there was a light ahead, a flashing light, and a familiar voice calling to him urgently across the darkness.

XIV

The Quality Of Mercy

The Public Schools Committee for Refugee Relief (Patroness: Sarah, Countess of Sawley) has an office in Belgrave Square. It is not at all clear whether this luxurious situation is designed to entice the wealthy or encourage the dispossessed—or, as some irreverent voices in Society whispered, to provide the Countess of Sawley with an inexpensive *pied-à-terre* in the West End of London. The business of assisting refugees has been suitably relegated to the south of the river, to one of those untended squares in Kennington which are part of London's architectural schizophrenia. York Gardens, as the square is called, will one day be discovered by the world, and its charm lost, but go there now, and you may see real children playing hopscotch in the road, and their mothers, shod in bedroom slippers, abusing them from doorways.

Miss Brimley, despatched on her way by Smiley's telephone call the previous morning, had the rare gift of speaking to children as if they were human beings, and thus discovered without difficulty the dilapidated, unnamed house which served the Committee as a collecting centre. With the assistance of seven small boys, she pulled on the bell and waited patiently. At last she heard the clatter of feet descending an uncarpeted staircase, and the door was opened by a very beautiful girl.

They looked at one another with approval for a moment.

"I'm sorry to be a nuisance," Miss Brimley began, "but a friend of mine in the country has asked me to make some enquiries about a parcel of clothes that was sent up a day or two ago. She's made rather a stupid mistake."

"Oh, goodness, how awful," said the girl pleasantly. "Would you like to come in? Everything's frightfully chaotic, I'm afraid, and there's nothing to sit on, but we can give you powdered coffee in a mug."

Miss Brimley followed her in, closing the door firmly on the seven children, who were edging gently forward in her wake. She was in the hall, and everywhere she looked there were parcels of every kind, some wrapped in jute with smart labels, some in brown paper, torn and clumsy, some in crates and laundry baskets, old suitcases and even an antiquated cabin trunk with a faded yellow label on it which read: "Not wanted on voyage."

The girl led the way upstairs to what was evidently the office, a large room containing a deal table littered with correspondence, and a kitchen chair. An oil stove sputtered in one corner, and an electric kettle was steaming in a melancholy way beside it.

"I'm sorry," said the girl as they entered the room, "but there just isn't anywhere to talk downstairs. I mean, one can't talk on one leg like Incas. Or isn't it Incas? Perhaps it's Afghans. However did you find us?"

"I went to your West End office first," Miss Brimley replied, "and they told me I should come and see you. I think they were rather cross. After that I relied on children. They always know the way. You are Miss Dawney, aren't you?"

"Lord, no. I'm the sort of daily help. Jill Dawney's gone to see the Customs people at Rotherhide—she'll be back at tea time if you want to see her."

"Gracious, my dear, I'm sure I shan't keep you two minutes. A friend of mine who lives in Carne— ("Goodness! How grand," said the girl) she's a sort of cousin really, but it's simpler to call her a friend, isn't

it?—gave an old grey dress to the refugee people last
Thursday and now she's convinced she left her brooch
pinned to the bodice. I'm sure she hasn't done anything
of the sort, mind you—she's a scatter-brain creature—
but she rang me yesterday morning in a dreadful state
and made me promise to come round at once and ask. I
couldn't come yesterday, unfortunately—tied to my little paper from dawn till dusk. But I gather you're a bit
behind, so it won't be too late?"

"Gosh, no! We're miles behind. That's all the stuff
downstairs, waiting to be unpacked and sorted. It comes
from the voluntary reps at each school—sometimes
boys and sometimes Staff—and they put all the clothes
together and send them up in big parcels, either by train
or ordinary mail, usually by train. We sort them here
before sending abroad."

"That's what I gathered from Jane. As soon as she
realised she'd made this mistake she got hold of the
woman doing the collecting and sending, but of course
it was too late. The parcel had gone."

"How frantic. . . . Do you know when the parcel
was sent off?"

"Yes. On Friday morning."

"From Carne? Train or post?"

Miss Brimley had been dreading this question, but
she made a guess:

"Post, I believe."

Darting past Miss Brimley, the girl foraged among
the pile of papers on her desk and finally produced a
stiff-backed exercise book with a label on it marked
"Ledger." Opening it at random, she whisked quickly
back and forth through the pages, licking the tip of one
finger now and then in a harassed sort of way.

"Wouldn't have arrived till yesterday at the earli-
est," she said. "We certainly won't have opened it yet.
Honestly, I don't know how we shall *ever* cope, and
with Easter coming up we shall just get worse and
worse. On top of that, half our stuff is rotting in the
Customs sheds—hullo, here we are!" She pushed the
ledger over to Miss Brimley, her slim finger pointing to

a pencilled entry in the central column: "Carne, parcel post, 27 lb."

"I wonder," said Miss Brimley, "whether you would mind awfully if we had a quick look inside?"

They went downstairs to the hall.

"It's not quite as hideous as it looks," the girl called over her shoulder. "All the Monday lot will be nearest the door."

"How do you know where they come from if you can't read the postmark?" asked Miss Brimley as the girl began to forage among the parcels.

"We issue the volunteer reps. with our printed labels. The labels have an originator's number on. In other cases we just ask them to write the name of the school in capitals on the outside. You see, we simply can't allow covering letters; it would be *too* desperate. When we get a parcel all we have to do is send off a printed card acknowledging with thanks receipt of a parcel of such and such a date weighing so and so much. People who aren't reps won't send parcels to this address, you see—they'll send to the advertised address in Belgrave Square."

"Does the system work?"

"No," replied the girl, "it doesn't. The reps either forget to use our labels or they run out and can't be bothered to tell us. Ten days later they ring up in a rage because they haven't had an acknowledgement. Reps. change, too, without letting us know, and the packing and labelling instructions don't get passed on. Sometimes the boys will suddenly decide to do it themselves, and no one tells them the way to go about it. Lady Sarah gets as mad as a snake if parcels turn up at Head Office—they all have to be carted over here for repacking and inventories."

"I see." Miss Brimley watched anxiously as the girl foraged among the parcels, still talking.

"Did you say your friend actually *taught* at Carne? She must be terribly grand. I wonder what the Prince is like: he looks rather soft in his photographs. My cousin went to Carne—he's an utter wet. Do you know what he told me? During Ascot week they all . . . Hello!

Here we are!" The girl stood up, a large square parcel in her arms, and carried it to a table which stood in the shadow of the staircase. Miss Brimley, standing beside her as she began carefully to untie the stout twine, looked curiously at the printed label. In its top left-hand corner was stamped the symbol which the Committee had evidently allocated to Carne: C4. After the four the letter B had been written in with ballpoint pen.

"What does the B mean?" asked Miss Brimley.

"Oh, that's a local arrangement at Carne. Miss D'Arcy's the rep there, but they've done so well recently that she co-opted a friend to help with despatch. When we acknowledge we always mention whether it was A or B. B must be terribly keen, whoever she is."

Miss Brimley forebore from enquiring what proportion of the parcels from Carne had originated from Miss D'Arcy, and what proportion from her anonymous assistant.

The girl removed the string and turned the parcel upside down in order to liberate the overlap of wrapping paper. As she did so Miss Brimley caught sight of a faint brown smudge, no more, about the size of a shilling, near the join. It was consistent with her essential rationalism that she should search for any explanation other than that which so loudly presented itself. The girl continued the work of unwrapping, saying suddenly: "I say, Carne was where they had that dreadful murder, wasn't it—that master's wife who got killed by the gypsy? It really *is* awful, isn't it, how much of that kind of thing goes on? Hm! Thought as much," she remarked, suddenly interrupting herself. She had removed the outer paper, and was about to unwrap the bundle inside when her attention was evidently arrested by the appearance of the inner parcel.

"What?" Miss Brimley said quickly.

The girl laughed. "Oh, only the packing," she said. "The C4Bs are usually so neat—quite the best we get. This is quite different. Not the same person at all. Must be a stand-in. I thought so from the outside."

"How can you be so sure?"

"Oh, it's like handwriting. We can tell." She

laughed again, and without more ado removed the last
wrapping. "Grey dress, you said, didn't you? Let's see."
With both hands she began picking clothes from the top
of the pile and laying them to either side. She was
nearly half way through when she exclaimed "Well,
honestly! They must be having a brain-storm," and
drew from the bundle of partworn clothes a transparent
plastic mackintosh, a very old pair of leather gloves,
and a pair of rubber overshoes.

Miss Brimley was holding the edge of the table
very tightly. The palms of her hands were throbbing.

"Here's a cape. Damp, too," the girl added in disgust, and tossed the offending articles on to the floor
beside the table. Miss Brimley could only think of Smiley's letter: "Whoever killed her must have been covered in blood." Yes, and whoever killed her wore a
plastic cape and a hood, rubber overshoes and those old
leather gloves with the terra-cotta stains. Whoever
killed Stella Rode had not chanced upon her in the
night, but had plotted long ahead, had waited. "Yes,"
thought Miss Brimley, "had waited for the long nights."

The girl was talking to her again: "I'm afraid it
really isn't here."

"No, my dear," Miss Brimley replied, "I see that.
Thank you. You've been very sweet." Her voice fal-
tered for a moment, then she managed to say: "I think,
my dear, you should leave the parcel exactly as it is
now, the wrapping and everything in it. Something very
dreadful has happened, and the police will want to . . .
know about it and see the parcel. . . . You must trust
me, my dear—things aren't quite what they seem. . . ."
And somehow she escaped to the comforting freedom of
York Gardens and the large-eyed wonder of its waiting
children.

She went to a telephone box. She got through to
the Sawley Arms and asked a very bored receptionist
for Mr. Smiley. Total silence descended on the line until
the Trunks operator asked her to put in another three
and sixpence. Miss Brimley replied sharply that all she

had so far had for her money was a three-minute vacuum; this was followed by the unmistakable sound of the operator sucking her teeth, and then, quite suddenly, by George Smiley's voice:

"George, it's Brim. A plastic mackintosh, a cape, rubber overshoes and some leather gloves that look as though they're stained with blood. Smudges on some of the wrapping paper too by the look of it."

A pause.

"Handwriting on the outside of the parcel?"

"None. The Charity organisers issue printed labels."

"Where is the stuff now? Have you got it?"

"No. I've told the girl to leave everything exactly as it is. It'll be all right for an hour or two. . . . George, are you there?"

"Yes."

"Who did it? Was it the husband?"

"I don't know. I just don't know."

"Do you want me to do anything—about the clothes, I mean? Phone Sparrow or anything?"

"No. I'll see Rigby at once. Goodbye, Brim. Thanks for ringing."

She put back the receiver. He sounded strange, she thought. He seemed to lose touch sometimes. As if he'd switched off.

She walked northwest towards the Embankment. It was long after ten o'clock—the first time she'd been late for Heaven knows how long. She had better take a taxi. Being a frugal woman, however, she took a bus.

Ailsa Brimley did not believe in emergencies, for she enjoyed a discipline of mind uncommon in men and even rarer in women. The greater the emergency, the greater her calm. John Landsbury had remarked upon it: "You have sales resistance to the dramatic, Brim; the rare gift of contempt for what is urgent. I know of a dozen people who would pay you five thousand a year for telling them everyday that what is important is seldom urgent. Urgent equals ephemeral, and ephemeral equals unimportant."

She got out of the bus, carefully putting the ticket in the rubbish compartment. As she stood in the warm sunlight of the street she caught sight of the hoardings advertising the first edition of the evening papers. If it hadn't been for the sun, she might never have looked; but the sun dazzled her and made her glance downwards. And so she did see; she read it in the plump black of the wet newsprint, in the prepacked hysteria of Fleet Street: "All-night search for missing Carne boy."

XV

The Road To Fielding

Smiley put down the receiver and walked quickly past the reception desk towards the front door. He must see Rigby at once. Just as he was leaving the hotel he heard his name called. Turning, he saw his old enemy, the night porter, braving the light of day, beckoning to him like Charon with his grey hand.

"They've been on to you from the police station," he observed with undisguised pleasure; "Mr. Rigby wants you, the Inspector. You're to go there at once. At once, see?"

"I'm on my way there now," Smiley replied irritably, and as he pushed his way through the swing doors he heard the old man repeat; "At once, mind; they're waiting for you."

Making his way through the Carne streets, he reflected for the hundredth time on the obscurity of motive in human action: there is no true thing on earth. There is no constant, no dependable point, not even in the purest logic or the most obscure mysticism; least of all in the motives of men when they are moved to act violently.

Had the murderer, now so near discovery, found contentment in the meticulous administration of his plans? For now it was clear beyond a doubt; this was a

113

murder devised to the last detail, even to the weapon inexplicably far from the place of its use; a murder with clues cast to mislead, a murder planned to look unplanned, a murder for a string of beads. Now the mystery of the footprints was solved: having put the overshoes into the parcel, the murderer had walked down the path to the gate, and his own prints had been obscured by the subsequent traffic of feet.

Rigby looked tired.

"You've heard the news, sir, I suppose?"

"What news?"

"About the boy, the boy in Fielding's house, missing all night?"

"No." Smiley felt suddenly sick. "No, I've heard nothing."

"Good Lord, I thought you knew! Half-past eight last night Fielding rang us here. Perkins, his head boy, hadn't come back from a music lesson with Mrs. Harlowe, who lives over to Longemede. We put out an alert and started looking for him. They sent a patrol car along the road he should have come back on—he was cycling, you see. The first time they didn't see anything, but on the way back the driver stopped the car at the bottom of Longemede Hill, just where the water-splash is. It occurred to him the lad might have taken a long run at the water-splash from the top of the hill, and come to grief in the dip. They found him half in the ditch, his bike beside him. Dead."

"Oh, my dear God."

"We didn't let on to the press at first. The boy's parents are in Singapore. The father's an Army officer. Fielding sent them a telegram. We've got on to the War Office, too."

They were silent for a moment, then Smiley asked "How did it happen?"

"We've closed the road and we've been trying to reconstruct the accident. I've got a detective over there now, just having a look. Trouble is, we couldn't do much till the morning. Besides, the men trampled everywhere; you can't blame them. It looks as though he must have fallen near the bottom of the hill and hit his head on a stone: his right temple."

"How did Fielding take it?"

"He was very shaken. Very shaken indeed. I wouldn't have believed it, to be quite honest. He just seemed to . . . give up. There was a lot that had to be done—telegraph the parents, get in touch with the boy's uncle at Windsor, and so on. But he just left all that to Miss Truebody, his housekeeper. If it hadn't been for her, I don't know how he'd have managed. I was with him for about half an hour, then he just broke down, completely, and asked to be left alone."

"How do you mean, broke down?" Smiley asked quickly.

"He cried. Wept like a child," said Rigby evenly. "I'd never have thought it."

Smiley offered Rigby a cigarette and took one himself.

"I suppose," he ventured, "it was an accident?"

"I suppose so," Rigby replied woodenly.

"Perhaps," said Smiley, "before we go any further, I'd better give you my news. I was on my way to see you when you rang. I've just heard from Miss Brimley." And in his precise, rather formal way he related all that Ailsa Brimley had told him, and how he had become curious about the contents of the parcel.

Smiley waited while Rigby telephoned to London. Almost mechanically, Rigby described what he wanted done: the parcel and its contents were to be collected and arrangements made to subject them immediately to forensic examination; the surfaces should be tested for fingerprints. He would be coming up to London himself with some samples of a boy's handwriting and an examination paper; he would want the opinion of a handwriting expert. No, he would be coming by train on the 4.25 from Carne, arriving at Waterloo at 8.05. Could a car be sent to the station to collect him? There was silence, then Rigby said testily, "All right, I'll take a ruddy taxi," and rang off rather abruptly. He looked at Smiley angrily for a moment, then grinned, plucked at his ear and said:

"Sorry, sir; getting a bit edgy." He indicated the far wall with his head and added, "Fighting on too many fronts, I suppose. I shall have to tell the Chief about that parcel, but he's out shooting at the moment—only pigeon, with a couple of friends, he won't be long—but I haven't mentioned your presence here in Carne, as a matter of fact, and if you don't mind I'll . . ."

"Of course," Smiley cut in quickly. "It's much simpler if you keep me out of it."

"I shall tell him it was just a routine enquiry. We shall have to mention Miss Brimley later . . . but there's no point in making things worse, is there?"

"No."

"I shall have to let Janie go, I suppose. . . . She was right, wasn't she? Silver wings in the moonlight."

"I wouldn't—no, I wouldn't let her go, Rigby," said Smiley with unaccustomed vehemence. "Keep her with you as long as you can possibly manage. No more accidents, for Heaven's sake. We've had enough."

"Then you don't believe Perkins' death was an accident?"

"Good Lord, no," cried Smiley suddenly, "and nor do you, do you?"

"I've put a detective on to it," Rigby replied coolly. "I can't take the case myself. I shall be needed on the Rode murder. The Chief will have to call the Yard in now; there'll be hell to pay I can tell you. He thought it was all over bar the shouting."

"And in the meantime?"

"In the meantime, sir, I'm going to do my damnedest to find out who killed Stella Rode."

"If," said Smiley slowly, "if you find fingerprints on that mackintosh, which I doubt, will you have anything . . . local . . . to compare them with?"

"We've got Rode's, of course, and Janie's."

"But not Fielding's?"

Rigby hesitated.

"As a matter of fact, we have," he said at last.

"From long ago. But nothing to do with this kind of thing."

"It was during the war," said Smiley. "His brother told me. Up in the North. It was hushed up, wasn't it?"

Rigby nodded. "So far as I heard, only the D'Arcys knew; and the Master, of course. It happened in the holidays—some Air Force boy. The Chief was very helpful. . . ."

Smiley shook hands with Rigby and made his way down the familiar pine staircase. He noticed again the vaguely institutional smell of floor polish and carbolic soap, like the smell at Fielding's house.

He walked slowly back towards the Sawley Arms. At the point where he should have turned left to his hotel, however, he hesitated, then seemed to change his mind. Slowly, almost reluctantly, he crossed the road to the Abbey Close, and walked along the southern edge towards Fielding's house. He looked worried, almost frightened.

XVI

A Taste For Music

Miss Truebody opened the door. The rims of her eyes were pink, as though she had been weeping.

"I wonder if I might see Mr. Fielding? To say goodbye."

She hesitated: "Mr. Fielding's very upset. I doubt whether he'll want to see anyone." He followed her into the hall and watched her go to the study door. She knocked, inclined her head, then gently turned the handle and let herself in. It was a long time before she returned. "He'll be out shortly," she said, without looking at him. "Will you take off your coat?" She waited while he struggled out of his overcoat, then took it from him and hung it beside the Van Gogh chair. They stood together in silence, both looking towards the study door.

Then, quite suddenly, Fielding was standing in the half-open doorway, unshaven and in his shirt-sleeves. "For Christ's sake," he said thickly. "What do you want?"

"I just wanted to say goodbye, Fielding, and to offer you my condolences."

Fielding looked at him hard for a moment; he was leaning heavily against the doorway; "Well, goodbye. Thank you for calling." He waved one hand vaguely in the air. "You needn't have bothered really, need you?"

he added rudely. "You could have sent me a card, couldn't you?"

"I could have done, yes; it just seemed so very tragic, when he was so near success."

"What do you mean? What the devil do you mean?"

"I mean in his work . . . the improvement. Simon Snow was telling me all about it. Amazing really, the way Rode brought him on."

A long silence, then Fielding spoke: "Goodbye, Smiley. Thanks for coming." He was turning back into the study as Smiley called:

"Not at all . . . not at all. I suppose poor Rode must have been bucked with those exam. results, too. I mean it was more or less a matter of life and death for Perkins, passing that exam., wasn't it? He wouldn't have got his remove next Half if he'd failed in science. They might have superannuated him, I suppose, even though he was head of the house; then he couldn't have sat for the Army. Poor Perkins, he had a lot to thank Rode for, didn't he? And you, too, Fielding, I'm sure. You must have helped him wonderfully . . . both of you did, you and Rode; Rode and Fielding. His parents ought to know that. They're rather hard up, I gather; the father's in the Army, isn't he, in Singapore? It must have been a great effort keeping the boy at Carne. It will comfort them to know how much was done for him, won't it, Fielding?"

Smiley was very pale. "You've heard the latest, I suppose," he continued. "About that wretched gypsy woman who killed Stella Rode? They've decided she's fit to plead. I suppose they'll hang her. That'll be the third death, won't it? You know, I'll tell you an odd thing—just between ourselves, Fielding. I don't believe she did it. Do you? I don't believe she did it at all."

He was not looking at Fielding. He had clasped his little hands tightly behind his back, and he stood with his shoulders bowed and his head inclined to one side, as though listening for an answer.

Fielding seemed to feel Smiley's words like a physical pain. Slowly he shook his head:

"No," he said. "No. Carne killed them; it was Carne. It could only happen here. It's the game we play: the exclusion game. Divide and rule!" He looked Smiley full in the face, and shouted: "Now for God's sake go! You've got what you want, haven't you? You can pin me on your little board, can't you?" And then, to Smiley's distress, he began sobbing in great uncontrollable gulps, holding his hand across his brow. He appeared suddenly grotesque, stemming the childish tears with his chalky hand, his cumbersome feet turned inwards. Gently, Smiley coaxed him back into the study, gently sat him before the dead fire. Then he began talking to him softly and with compassion.

"If what I think is true, there isn't much time," he began. "I want you to tell me about Tim Perkins—about the exam."

Fielding, his face buried in his hands, nodded.

"He would have failed, wouldn't he? He would have failed and not got his Remove; he'd have had to leave." Fielding was silent. "After the exam. that day, Rode gave him the writing case to bring here, the case that contained the papers; Rode was doing chapel duty that week and wouldn't be going home before dinner, but he wanted to correct the papers that night, after his dinner with you."

Fielding took his hands from his face and leant back in his chair, his great head tilted back, his eyes closed. Smiley continued:

"Perkins came home, and that evening he brought the case to you, as Rode told him to, for safe keeping. Perkins, after all, was head of your house, a responsible boy. . . . He gave you the case and you asked him how he'd done in the exam."

"He wept," said Fielding suddenly. "He wept as only a child can."

"And after breaking down he told you he had cheated? That he had looked up the answers and copied them on to his paper. Is that right? And after the murder of Stella Rode he remembered what else he had seen in the suitcase?"

Fielding was standing up. "No! Don't you see?

Tim wouldn't have cheated to save his life! That's the whole point, the whole bloody irony of it," he shouted. "He never cheated at all. *I* cheated for him."

"But you couldn't! You couldn't copy his handwriting!"

"He wrote with a ball-pen. It was only formulae and diagrams. When he'd gone, and left me alone with the case, I looked at his paper. It was hopeless—he'd only done two out of seven questions. So I cheated for him. I just cribbed them from the science book, and wrote them with blue ballpoint, the kind we all use. Abbots' sell them. I copied his hand as best I could. It only needed about three lines of figures. The rest was diagrams."

"Then it was you who opened the case? You who saw . . ."

"Yes. It was me, I tell you, not Tim! He couldn't cheat to save his life! But Tim paid for it, don't you see? When the marks were published Tim must have known something was wrong with them. After all, he'd only attempted two questions out of seven and yet he'd got sixty-one per cent. But he knew *nothing* else, *nothing!*"

For a long time neither spoke. Fielding was standing over Smiley, exultant with the relief of sharing his secret, and Smiley was looking vaguely past him, his face drawn in deep concentration.

"And of course," he said finally, "when Stella was murdered, you knew who had done it."

"Yes," replied Fielding. "I knew that Rode had killed her."

Fielding poured himself a brandy and gave one to Smiley. He seemed to have recovered his self-control. He sat down and looked at Smiley thoughtfully for a time.

"I've got no money," he said at last. "None. Nobody knows that except the Master. Oh, they know I'm more or less broke, but they don't know *how* broke. Long ago I made an ass of myself. I got into trouble. It was in the war, when staff was impossible. I had a boys' house and was practically running the school—D'Arcy and I. We were running it together, and the Master running us. Then I made an ass of myself. It was during the holidays. I was up North at the time, giving a course of talks at an R.A.F. educational place. And I stepped out of line. Badly. They pulled me in. And along came D'Arcy wearing his country overcoat and bringing the Master's terms: Come back to Carne, my dear fellow, and we'll say no more about it; go on running your house, my dear fellow, and giving of your wisdom. There's been no publicity. We know it will never happen again, my dear fellow, and we're dreadfully hard up for staff. Come back as a temporary. So I did, and I've been one ever since, going cap in hand to darling D'Arcy every December asking for my contract to be renewed. And, of course—no pension. I shall have to teach at a crammer's. There's a place in Somerset where they'll take me. I'm seeing their Headmaster in London on Thursday. It's a sort of breaker's yard for old dons. The Master had to know, because he gave me a reference."

"That was why you couldn't tell anyone? Because of Perkins?"

"In a way, yes. I mean they'd want to know all sorts of things. I did it for Tim, you see. The Governors wouldn't have liked that much . . . inordinate affection. . . . It looks bad, doesn't it? But it wasn't that kind of affection, Smiley, not any more. You never heard him play the 'cello. He wasn't marvellous, but just sometimes he would play so beautifully, with a kind of studious simplicity, that was indescribably good. He was an awkward boy, and when he played well it was such a surprise. You should have heard him play."

"You didn't want to drag him into it. If you told the police what you had seen it would ruin Tim too?"

Fielding nodded. "In the whole of Carne, he was the one thing I loved."

"Loved?" asked Smiley.

"For God's sake," said Fielding in an exhausted voice, "why not?"

"His parents wanted him to go to Sandhurst; I didn't, I'm afraid. I thought that if I could keep him here another Half or two I might be able to get him a music scholarship. That's why I made him Head of House: I wanted his parents to keep him on because he was doing so well." Fielding paused; "He was a rotten Head of House," he added.

"And what exactly was in the writing-case," Smiley asked, "when you opened it that evening to look at Tim's exam. paper?"

"A sheet of transparent plastic . . . it may have been one of those pack-away cape things—an old pair of gloves, and a pair of home-made galoshes."

"Home-made?"

"Yes. Hacked from a pair of wellington boots, I should think."

"That's all?"

"No. There was a length of heavy cable, I presumed for demonstrating something in his science lessons. It seemed natural enough in winter to carry waterproofs about. Then, after the murder, I realised how he had done it."

"Did you know," asked Smiley, "*why* he had done it?"

Fielding seemed to hesitate: "Rode's a guinea-pig," he began, "the first man we've had from a grammar school. Most of us are old Carnians ourselves, in fact. Focused when we start. Rode wasn't, and Carne thrilled him. The very name Carne means quality, and Rode loved quality. His wife wasn't like that. She had her standards and they were different, but just as good. I used to watch Rode in the Abbey sometimes on Sunday mornings. Tutors sit at the end of pews, right by the aisle, you know. I used to watch his face as the choir processed past him in white and scarlet, and the Master in his doctor's robes and the Governors and Guardians behind him. Rode was drunk—drunk with the pride of Carne. We're heady wine for the grammar school men, you know. It must have hurt him terribly that Stella wouldn't share any of that. You could see it did. The night they came to dinner with me, the night she died, they argued. I never told anyone, but they did. The Master had preached a sermon at Compline that evening: 'Hold fast to that which is good.' Rode talked about it at dinner; he couldn't take much drink, you know, he wasn't used to it. He was full of this sermon and of the eloquence of the Master. She never came to the Abbey—she went to that drab tabernacle by the station. He went on and on about the beauty of the Abbey service, the dignity, the reverence. She kept quiet till he'd finished, then laughed, and said: 'Poor old Stan. You'll always be Stan to me.' I've never seen anyone so angry as he was then. He went quite pale."

Fielding swept his white hair from his eyes and went on, with something like the old panache: "I've watched her, too, at meals. Not just here, but at dinner parties elsewhere, when we've both been invited. I've watched her do the simplest things—like eating an apple. She'd peel it in one piece, round and round till the whole peel fell off. Then she'd cut the apple and dice the quarters, getting it all ready before she ate it. She might have been a miner's wife preparing it for her husband. She must have *seen* how people do things here, but it never occurred to her that she ought to copy them. I admire that. So do you, I expect. But Carne doesn't—and Rode didn't; above all, Rode didn't. He'd watch her, and I think he grew to hate her for not conforming. He came to see her as the bar to his success, the one factor which would deprive him of a great career. Once he'd reached that conclusion, what could he do? He couldn't divorce her—that would do him more harm than remaining married to her. Rode knew what Carne would think of divorce; we're a Church foundation, remember. So he killed her. He plotted a squalid murder, and with his little scientist's mind he gave them all the clues they wanted. Fabricated clues. Clues that would point to a murderer who didn't exist. But something went wrong; Tim Perkins got sixty-one per cent. He'd got an impossible mark—he must have cheated. He'd had the opportunity—he'd had the papers in the case. Rode put his little mind to it and decided what had happened: Tim had opened the case and he'd seen the cape and the boots and the gloves. And the cable. So Rode killed him too."

With surprising energy, Fielding got up and gave himself more brandy. His face was flushed, almost exultant.

Smiley stood up. "When did you say you'll be coming to London? Thursday, wasn't it?"

"Yes. I had arranged to lunch with my crammer man at one of those dreadful clubs in Pall Mall. I always go into the wrong one, don't you? But I'm afraid there's not much point in my seeing him now, is there, if all this is going to come out? Not even a crammer's will take me then."

Smiley hesitated.

"Come and dine with me that evening. Spend the night if you want. I'll ask one or two other people. We'll have a party. You'll feel better by then. We can talk a bit. I might be able to help you . . . for Adrian's sake."

"Thank you. I should like to. Interview apart, I've got some odds and ends to clear up in London, anyway."

"Good. Quarter to eight. Bywater Street, Chelsea, number 9A." Fielding wrote it down in his diary. His hand was quite steady.

"Black tie?" asked Fielding, his pen poised, and some imp made Smiley reply:

"I usually do, but it doesn't matter." There was a moment's silence.

"I suppose," Fielding began tentatively, "that all this *will* come out in the trial, about Tim and me? I'll be ruined if it does, you know, ruined."

"I don't see how they can prevent it."

"I feel much better now, anyway," said Fielding; "much."

With a cursory goodbye, Smiley left him alone. He walked quickly back to the police station, reasonably confident that Terence Fielding was the most accomplished liar he had met for a long time.

XVII

Rabbit Run

He knocked on Rigby's door and walked straight in.

"I'm awfully afraid you'll have to arrest Stanley Rode," he began, and recounted his interview with Fielding.

"I shall have to tell the Chief," said Rigby doubtfully. "Would you like to repeat all that in front of him? If we're going to pull in a Carne master, I think the Chief had better know first. He's just come back. Hang on a minute." He picked up the telephone on his desk and asked for the Chief Constable. A few minutes later they were walking in silence down a carpeted corridor. On either wall hung photographs of rugby and cricket teams, some yellow and faded from the Indian sun, others done in a sepia tint much favoured by Carne photographers in the early part of the century. At intervals along the corridor stood empty buckets of brilliant red, with FIRE printed carefully in white on the outside. At the far end of the corridor was a dark oak door. Rigby knocked and waited. There was silence. He knocked again and was answered with a cry of "Come!"

Two very large spaniels watched them come in. Behind the spaniels, at an enormous desk, Brigadier Havelock, O.B.E., Chief Constable of Carne, sat like a water rat on a raft.

The few strands of white hair which ran laterally

across his otherwise bald head were painstakingly adjusted to cover the maximum area. This gave him an oddly wet look, as if he had just emerged from the river. His moustache, which lavishly compensated for the scarcity of other hair, was yellow and appeared quite solid. He was a very small man, and he wore a brown suit and a stiff white collar with rounded corners.

"Sir," Rigby began, "may I introduce Mr. Smiley from London?"

He came out from behind his desk as if he were giving himself up, unconvinced but resigned. Then he pushed out a little, knobbly hand and said, "From London, eh? How d'you do, sir," all at once, as if he'd learnt it by heart.

"Mr. Smiley's here on a private visit, sir," Rigby continued. "He is an acquaintance of Mr. Fielding."

"Quite a card, Fielding, quite a card," the Chief Constable snapped.

"Yes, indeed, sir," said Rigby, and went on:

"Mr. Smiley called on Mr. Fielding just now, sir, to take his leave before returning to London." Havelock shot a beady glance at Smiley, as if wondering whether he were fit to make the journey.

"Mr. Fielding made a kind of statement, which he substantiated with new evidence of his own. About the murder, sir."

"Well, Rigby?" he said challengingly. Smiley intervened:

"He said that the husband had done it; Stanley Rode. Fielding said that when his head boy brought him Rode's writing-case containing the examination papers . . ."

"What examination papers?"

"Rode was invigilating that afternoon, you remember. He was also doing chapel duty before going on to dinner at Fielding's house. As an expediency, he gave the papers to Perkins to take . . ."

"The boy who had the accident?" Havelock asked. "Yes."

"You know a lot about it," said Havelock darkly.

"Fielding said that when Perkins brought him the

case, Fielding opened it. He wanted to see how Perkins had done in the science paper. It was vital to the boy's future that he should get his Remove," Smiley went on.

"Oh, work's the only thing now," said Havelock bitterly. "Wasn't the way when I was a boy here, I assure you."

"When Fielding opened the case, the papers were inside. So was a plastic cape, an old pair of leather gloves and a pair of rubber overshoes, cut from wellingtons."

A pause.

"Good God! Good God! Hear that, Rigby? That's what they found in the parcel in London. Good God!"

"Finally, there was a length of cable, heavy cable, in the case as well. It was this writing-case that Rode went back for, you remember, on the night of the murder," Smiley concluded. It was like feeding a child—you couldn't overload the spoon.

There was a very long silence indeed. Then Rigby, who seemed to know his man, said:

"Motive was self-advancement in the profession, sir. Mrs. Rode showed no desire to improve her station, dressed in a slovenly manner and took no part in the religious life of the school."

"Just a minute," said Havelock. "Rode planned the murder from the start, correct?"

"Yes, sir."

"He wanted to make it look like robbery with violence."

"Yes, sir."

"Having collected the writing-case, he walked back to North Fields. Then what does he do?"

"He puts on the plastic cape and hood, overshoes and gloves. He arms himself with the weapon, sir. He lets himself in by the garden gate, crosses the back garden, goes to the front door and rings the bell, sir. His wife comes to the door. He knocks her down, drags her to the conservatory and murders her. He rinses the clothes under the tap and puts them in the parcel. Having sealed the parcel, he walks down the drive this time to the front gate, following the path, sir, knowing that his own footprints will soon be obscured by other people's. Having got to the road, where the snow was hard and showed no prints, he turned round and re-entered the house, playing the part of the distressed husband, taking care, when he discovers the body, sir, to put his own fingerprints over the glove-marks. There was one article that was too dangerous to send, sir. The weapon."

"All right, Rigby. Pull him in. Mr. Borrow will give you a warrant if you want one; otherwise I'll ring Lord Sawley."

"Yes, sir. And I'll send Sergeant Low to take a full statement from Mr. Fielding, sir?"

"Why the devil didn't he speak up earlier, Rigby?"

"Have to ask him that, sir," said Rigby woodenly, and left the room.

"You a Carnian?" Havelock asked, pushing a silver cigarette-box across the desk.

"No. No, I'm afraid not," Smiley replied.

"How d'you know Fielding?"

"We met at Oxford after the war."

"Queer card, Fielding, very queer. Say your name was Smiley?"

"Yes."

"There was a fellow called Smiley married Ann Sercombe, Lord Sawley's cousin. Damned pretty girl, Ann was, and went and married this fellow. Some funny little beggar in the Civil Service with an O.B.E. and a gold watch. Sawley was damned annoyed." Smiley said nothing. "Sawley's got a son at Carne. Know that?"

"I read it in the press, I think."

"Tell me—this fellow Rode. He's a grammar school chap, isn't he?"

"I believe so, yes."

"Damned odd business. Experiments never pay, do they. You can't experiment with tradition."

"No. No, indeed."

"That's the trouble today. Like Africa. Nobody

seems to understand you can't build society overnight. It takes centuries to make a gentleman." Havelock frowned to himself and fiddled with the paper-knife on his desk.

"Wonder how he got his cable into that ditch, the thing he killed her with. He wasn't out of our sight for forty-eight hours after the murder."

"That," said Smiley, "is what puzzles me. So does Jane Lyn."

"What d'you mean?"

"I don't believe Rode would have had the nerve to walk back to the house after killing his wife knowing that Jane Lyn had seen him do it. Assuming, of course, that he *did* know, which seems likely. It's too cool . . . too cool altogether."

"Odd, damned odd," muttered Havelock. He looked at his watch, pushing his left elbow outwards to do so, in a swift equestrian movement which Smiley found comic, and a little sad. The minutes ticked by. Smiley wondered if he should leave, but he had a vague feeling that Havelock wanted his company.

"There'll be a hell of a fuss," said Havelock. "It isn't every day you arrest a Carne tutor for murder." He put down the paper-knife sharply on the desk.

"These bloody journalists ought to be horse-whipped!" he declared. "Look at the stuff they print about the Royal Family. Wicked, wicked!" He got up, crossed the room and sat himself in a leather armchair by the fire. One of the spaniels went and sat at his feet.

"What made him do it, I wonder. What the devil made him do it? His own wife, I mean; a fellow like that." Havelock said this simply, appealing for enlightenment.

"I don't believe," said Smiley slowly, "that we can ever entirely know what makes anyone do anything."

"My God, you're dead right. . . . What do you do for a living, Smiley?"

"After the war I was at Oxford for a bit. Teaching and research. I'm in London now."

"One of those clever coves, eh?"

Smiley wondered when Rigby would return.

"Know anything about this fellow's family? Has he got people, or anything?"

"I think they're both dead," Smiley answered, and the telephone on Havelock's desk rang sharply. It was Rigby. Stanley Rode had disappeared.

XVIII

After The Ball

He caught the 1.30 train to London. He just made it after an argument at his hotel about the bill. He left a note for Rigby giving his address and telephone number in London and asking him to telephone that night when the laboratory tests were completed. There was nothing else for him to do in Carne.

As the train pulled slowly out of Carne and one by one the familiar landmarks disappeared into the cold February mist, George Smiley was filled with a feeling of relief. He hadn't wanted to come, he knew that. He'd been afraid of the place where his wife had spent her childhood, afraid to see the fields where she had lived. But he had found nothing, not the faintest memory, neither in the lifeless outlines of Sawley Castle, nor in the surrounding countryside, to remind him of her. Only the gossip remained, as it would while the Hechts and the Havelocks survived to parade their acquaintance with the first family in Carne.

He took a taxi to Chelsea, carried his suitcase upstairs and unpacked with the care of a man accustomed to living alone. He thought of having a bath, but decided to ring Ailsa Brimley first. The telephone was by his bed. He sat on the edge of the bed and dialled the number. A tinny model-voice sang: "Unipress, good afternoon," and he asked for Miss Brimley. There was a

long silence, then, "Ah'm afraid Miss Brimley is in conference. Can someone else answer your query?"

Query, thought Smiley. Good God! Why on earth
query—why not question or enquiry?

"No," he replied. "Just tell her Mr. Smiley rang."
He put back the receiver and went into the bathroom
and turned on the hot tap. He was fiddling with his
cuff-links when the telephone rang. It was Ailsa Brimley:

"George? I think you'd better come round at once.
We've got a visitor. Mr. Rode from Carne. He wants to
talk to us." Pulling on his jacket, he ran out into the
street and hailed a taxi.

XIX

Disposal Of A Legend

The descending escalator was packed with the staff of Unipress, homebound and heavy-eyed. To them, the sight of a fat, middle-aged gentleman bounding up the adjoining staircase provided unexpected entertainment, so that Smiley was hastened on his way by the jeers of officeboys and the laughter of typists. On the first floor he paused to study an enormous board carrying the titles of a quarter of the national dailies. Finally, under the heading of "Technical and Miscellaneous," he spotted the *Christian Voice*, Room 619. The lift seemed to go up very slowly. Formless music issued from behind its plush, while a boy in a monkey jacket flicked his hips on the heavier beats. The golden doors parted with a sigh, the boy said "Six," and Smiley stepped quickly into the corridor. A moment or two later he was knocking on the door of Room 619. It was opened by Ailsa Brimley.

"George, how nice," she said brightly. "Mr. Rode will be dreadfully pleased to see you." And without any further introduction she led him into her office. In an armchair near the window sat Stanley Rode, tutor of Carne, in a neat black overcoat. As Smiley entered he stood up and held out his hand. "Good of you to come, sir," he said woodenly. "Very." The same flat manner, the same cautious voice.

"How can I help you?" asked Smiley.

They all sat down. Smiley offered Miss Brimley a cigarette and lit it for her.

"It's about this article you're writing about Stella," he began. "I feel awful about it really, because you've been so good to her, and her memory, if you see what I mean. I know you wish well, but I don't want you to write it."

Smiley said nothing, and Ailsa was wise enough to keep quiet. From now on it was Smiley's interview. The silence didn't worry him, but it seemed to worry Rode.

"It wouldn't be right; it wouldn't do at all. Mr. Glaston agreed; I spoke to him yesterday before he left and he agreed. I just couldn't let you write that stuff."

"Why not?"

"Too many people know, you see. Poor Mr. Cardew, I asked him. He knows a lot; and a lot about Stella, so I asked him. He understands why I gave up Chapel too; I couldn't bear to see her going there every Sunday and going down on her knees." He shook his head. "It was all wrong. It just made a fool of your faith."

"What did Mr. Cardew say?"

"He said we should not be the judges. We should let God judge. But I said to him it wouldn't be right, those people knowing her and knowing what she'd done, and then reading all that stuff in the *Voice*. They'd think it was crazy. He didn't seem to see that, he just said to leave it to God. But I can't, Mr. Smiley."

Again no one spoke for a time. Rode sat quite still, save for a very slight rocking movement of his head. Then he began to talk again:

"I didn't believe old Mr. Glaston at first. He said she was bad, but I didn't believe it. They lived up on the hill then, Gorse Hill, only a step from the Tabernacle; Stella and her father. They never seemed to keep servants for long, so she did most of the work. I used to call in Sunday mornings sometimes after church. Stella looked after her father, cooked for him and everything, and I always wondered how I'd ever have the nerve to ask Mr. Glaston for her. The Glastons were big people in Branxome. I was teaching at Grammar School in those days. They let me teach part-time while I read for my degree, and I made up my mind that if I passed the exam, I'd ask her to marry me.

"The Sunday after the results came out I went round to the house after morning service. Mr. Glaston opened the door himself. He took me straight into the study. You could see half the potteries in Poole from the window, and the sea beyond. He sat me down and he said: 'I know what you're here for, Stanley. You want to marry Stella. But you don't know her,' he said, 'you don't know her.' 'I've been visiting two years, Mr. Glaston,' I said, 'and I think I know my mind.' Then he started talking about her. I never thought to hear a human being talk like that of his own child. He said she was bad—bad in her heart. That she was full of malice. That was why no servants would stay at the Hill. He told me how she'd lead people on, all kind and warm, till they'd told her everything, then she'd hurt them, saying wicked, wicked things, half true, half lies. He told me a lot more besides, and I didn't believe it, not a word. I think I lost my head; I called him a jealous old man who didn't want to lose his housekeeper, a lying, jealous old man who wanted his child to wait on him till he died. I said it was him who was bad, not Stella, and I shouted at him liar, liar. He didn't seem to hear, just shook his head, and I ran out into the hall and called Stella. She'd been in the kitchen, I think, and she came to me and put her arms round me and kissed me.

"We were married a month later, and the old man gave her away. He shook my hand at the wedding and called me a fine man, and I thought what an old hypocrite he was. He gave us money—to me, not her—two thousand pounds. I thought perhaps he was trying to make up for the dreadful things he'd said, and later I wrote to him and said I forgave him. He never answered and I didn't see him often after that.

"For a year or more we were happy enough at Branxome. She was just what I thought she'd be, neat and simple. She liked to go for walks and kiss at the stiles; she liked to be a bit grand sometimes, going to the Dolphin for dinner all dressed up. It meant a lot to me then, I don't mind admitting, going to the right places with Mr. Glaston's daughter. He was Rotary and on the Council and quite a figure in Branxome. She used to tease me about it—in front of other people too, which got me a bit. I remember one time we went to the Dolphin, one of the waiters there was a bloke called Johnnie Raglan. We'd been to school together. Johnnie was a bit of a tear-about and hadn't done anything much since he'd left school except run after girls and get into trouble. Stella knew him, I don't know how, and she waved to him as soon as we'd sat down. Johnnie came over and Stella made him bring another chair and sit with us. The Manager looked daggers, but he didn't dare to do anything because she was Samuel Glaston's daughter. Johnnie stayed there all the meal and Stella talked to him about school and what I was like. Johnnie was pleased as punch and got cheeky, saying I'd been a swat and a good boy and all the rest, and how Johnnie had knocked me about—lies most of it, and she egged him on. I went for her afterwards and said I didn't pay good money at the Dolphin to hear Johnnie Raglan tell a lot of tall stories, and she turned on me fast like a cat. It was her money, she said, and Johnnie was as good as me any day. Then she was sorry and kissed me and I pretended to forgive her."

Sweat was forming on his face; he was talking fast, the words tripping over each other. It was like a man recalling a nightmare, as if the memory were still there, the fear only half gone. He paused and looked sharply at Smiley as if expecting him to speak, but Smiley seemed to be looking past him, his face impassive, its soft contours grown hard.

"Then we went to Carne. I'd just started reading *The Times* and I saw the advert. They wanted a science tutor and I applied. Mr. D'Arcy interviewed me and I got the job. It wasn't till we got to Carne that I knew that what her father had said was true. She hadn't been very keen on Chapel before, but as soon as she got here

she went in for it in a big way. She knew it would look
wrong, that it would hurt me. Branxome's a fine big
church, you see; there was nothing funny about going to
Branxome Tabernacle. But at Carne it was different;
Carne Tabernacle's a little out-of-the-way place with a
tin roof. She wanted to be different, to spite the school
and me, by playing the humble one. I wouldn't have
minded if she'd been sincere, but she wasn't, Mr. Cardew knew that. He got to know Stella, Mr. Cardew did.
I think her father told him; anyway, Mr. Cardew was
up North before, and he knew the family well. For all I
know he wrote to Mr. Glaston, or went and saw him or
something.

"She began there well enough. The townspeople
were all pleased enough to see her—a wife from the
School coming to the Tabernacle, that had never happened before. Then she took to running the appeal for
the refugees—to collecting clothes and all that. Miss
D'Arcy was running it for the school, Mr. D'Arcy's sister, and Stella wanted to beat her at her own game—to
get more from the Chapel people than Miss D'Arcy got
from the School. But I knew what she was doing, and so
did Mr. Cardew, and so did the townspeople in the end.
She listened. Every drop of gossip and dirt, she hoarded
it away. She'd come home of an evening sometimes—
Wednesdays and Fridays she did her Chapel work—and
she'd throw off her coat and laugh till I thought she'd
gone mad.

"'I've got them! I've got them all,' she'd say. 'I
know all their little secrets and I've got them in the hol-
low of my hand, Stan.' That's what she'd say. And those
that realised grew to be frightened of her. They all gossiped, Heaven knows, but not to profit from it, not like
Stella. Stella was cunning; anything decent, anything
good, she'd drag it down and spoil it. There were a
dozen she'd got the measure of. There was Mulligan the
furniture man; he's got a daughter with a kid near
Leamington. Somehow she found out the girl wasn't
married—they'd sent her to an aunt to have her baby
and begin again up there. She rang up Mulligan once,
something to do with a bill for moving Simon Snow's

furniture, and she said 'Greetings from Leamington Spa, Mr. Mulligan. We need a little co-operation.' She told me that—she came home laughing her head off and told me. But they got her in the end, didn't they? They got their own back!"

Smiley nodded slowly, his eyes now turned fully upon Rode.

"Yes," he said at last, "they got their own back."

"They thought Mad Janie did it, but I didn't. Janie'd as soon have killed her own sister as Stella. They were as close as moon and stars, that's what Stella said. They'd talk together for hours in the evenings when I was out late on Societies or Extra Tuition. Stella cooked food for her, gave her clothes and money. It gave her a feeling of power to help a creature like Janie, and have her fawning round. Not because she was kind, but because she was cruel.

"She'd brought a little dog with her from Branxome, a mongrel. One day a few months ago I came home and found it lying in the garage whimpering, terrified. It was limping and had blood on its back. She'd beaten it. She must have gone mad. I knew she'd beaten it before, but never like that; never. Then something happened—I shouted at her and she laughed and then I hit her. Not hard, but hard enough. In the face. I gave her twenty-four hours to have the dog destroyed or I'd tell the police. She screamed at me—it was her dog and she'd damn' well do what she liked with it—but next day she put on her little black hat and took the dog to the vet. I suppose she told him some tale. She could spin a good tale about anything, Stella could. She kind of stepped into a part and played it right through. Like the tale she told the Hungarians. Miss D'Arcy had some refugees to stay from London once and Stella told them such a tale they ran away and had to be taken back to London. Miss D'Arcy paid for their fares and everything, even had the welfare officer down to see them and try and put things right. I don't think Miss D'Arcy ever knew who'd got at them, but I did—Stella told me. She laughed, always that same laugh: 'There's your fine lady, Stan. Look at her charity now.'

"After the dog, she took to pretending I was violent, cringing away whenever I came near, holding her arm up as though I was going to hit her again. She even made out I was plotting to murder her: she went and told Mr. Cardew I was. She didn't believe it herself; she'd laugh about it sometimes. She said to me: 'It's no good killing me now, Stan; they'll all know who's done it.' But other times she'd whine and stroke me, begging me not to kill her. 'You'll kill me in the long nights!' She'd scream it out—it was the words that got her, the long nights, she liked the sound of them the way an actor does, and she'd build a whole story round them. 'Oh, Stan,' she'd say, 'keep me safe in the long nights.' You know how it is when you never meant to do anything anyway, and someone goes on begging you not to do it? You think you might do it after all, you begin to consider the possibility."

Miss Brimley drew in her breath rather quickly. Smiley stood up and walked over to Rode.

"Why don't we go back to my house for some food?" he said. "We can talk this over quietly. Among friends."

They took a taxi to Bywater Street. Rode sat beside Ailsa Brimley, more relaxed now, and Smiley, opposite him on a drop-seat, watched him and wondered. And it occurred to him that the most important thing about Rode was that he had no friends. Smiley was reminded of Büchner's fairy tale of the child left alone in an empty world who, finding no one to talk to, went to the moon because it smiled at him, but the moon was made of rotten wood. And when the sun and moon and stars had all turned to nothing, he tried to go back to the earth, but it had gone.

Perhaps because Smiley was tired, or perhaps because he was getting a little old, he felt a movement of sudden compassion towards Rode, such as children feel for the poor and parents for their children. Rode had tried so hard—he had used Carne's language, bought the right clothes, and thought as best he could the right thoughts, yet remained hopelessly apart, hopelessly alone.

He lit the gas-fire in the drawing room while Ailsa Brimley went to the delicatessen in the King's Road for soup and eggs. He poured out whisky and soda and gave one to Rode, who drank it in short sips, without speaking.

"I had to tell somebody," he said at last. "I thought you'd be a good person. I didn't want you to print that article, though. Too many knew, you see."

"How many really knew?"

"Only those she'd gone for, I think. I suppose about a dozen townspeople. And Mr. Cardew, of course. She was terribly cunning, you see. She didn't often pass on gossip. She knew to a hair how far she could go. Those who knew were the ones she'd got on the hook. Oh, and D'Arcy, Felix D'Arcy, he knew. She had something special there, something she never told me about. There were nights when she'd put on her shawl and slip out, all excited as if she was going to a party. Quite late sometimes, eleven or twelve. I'd never ask her where she was going because it only bucked her, but sometimes she'd nod at me all cunning and say, 'You don't know, Stan, but D'Arcy does. D'Arcy knows and he can't tell,' and then she'd laugh again and try and look mysterious, and off she'd go."

Smiley was silent for a long time, watching Rode and thinking. Then he asked suddenly: "What was Stella's blood group, do you know?"

"Mine's B. I know that. I was a donor at Branxome. Hers was different."

"How do you know that?"

"She had a test before we were married. She used to suffer from anaemia. I remember hers being different, that's all. Probably A. I can't remember for sure. Why?"

"Where were you registered as a donor?"

"North Poole Transfusion Centre."

"Will they know you there still? Are you still recorded there?"

"I suppose so."

The front door bell rang. It was Ailsa Brimley, back from her shopping.

Ailsa installed herself in the kitchen, while Rode and Smiley sat in the warm comfort of the drawing-room.

"Tell me something else," said Smiley, "about the night of the murder. Why did you leave the writing-case behind? Was it absent-mindedness?"

"No, not really. I was on Chapel duty that night, so Stella and I arrived separately at Fielding's house. She got there before I did and I think Fielding gave the case to her—right at the start of the evening so that it wouldn't get forgotten. He said something about it later that evening. She'd put the case beside her coat in the hall. It was only a little thing about eighteen inches by twelve. I could have sworn she was carrying it as we stood in the hall saying goodbye, but I must have been mistaken. It wasn't till we got to the house that she asked me what I'd done with it."

"*She* asked *you* what you'd done with it?"

"Yes. Then she threw a temper and said I expected her to remember everything. I didn't particularly want to go back, I could have rung Fielding and arranged to collect it first thing next morning, but Stella wouldn't hear of it. She made me go. I didn't like to tell the police all this stuff about us quarrelling, it didn't seem right."

Smiley nodded. "When you got back to Fielding's you rang the bell?"

"Yes. There's the front door, then a glass door inside, a sort of french window to keep out draughts. The front door was still open, and the light was on in the hall. I rang the bell and collected the case from Fielding."

They had finished supper when the telephone rang.

"Rigby here, Mr. Smiley. I've got the laboratory results. They're rather puzzling."

"The exam. paper first: it doesn't tally?"

"No, it doesn't. The boffins here say all the figures and writing were done with the same ballpoint pen. They can't be sure about the diagrams but they say the legend on all the diagrams corresponds to the rest of the script on the sheet."

"All done by the boy after all in fact?"

"Yes. I brought up some other samples of his handwriting for comparison. They match the exam. paper right the way through. Fielding couldn't have tinkered with it."

"Good. And the clothing? Nothing there either?"

"Traces of blood, that's all. No prints on the plastic."

"What was her blood group, by the way?"

"Group A."

Smiley sat down on the edge of the bed. Pressing the receiver to his ear, he began talking quietly. Ten minutes later he was walking slowly downstairs. He had come to the end of the chase, and was already sickened by the kill.

It was nearly an hour before Rigby arrived.

XX

The Dross Of The River

Albert Bridge was as preposterous as ever; bony steel, rising to Wagnerian pinnacles, against the patient London sky; the Thames crawling beneath it with resignation, edging its filth into the wharves of Battersea, then sliding towards the mist down river.

The mist was thick. Smiley watched the driftwood, as it touched it, turning first to white dust, then seeming to lift, dissolve and vanish.

This was how it would end, on a foul morning like this when they dragged the murderer whimpering from his cell and put the hempen rope round his neck. Would Smiley have the courage to recall this two months from now, as the dawn broke outside his window and the clock rang out the time? When they broke a man's neck on the scaffold and put him away like the dross of the river?

He made his way along Beaumont Street towards the King's Road. The milkman chugged past him in his electric van. He would breakfast out this morning, then take a cab to Curzon Street and order the wine for dinner. He would choose something good. Fielding would like that.

Fielding closed his eyes and drank, his left hand held lightly across his chest.

"Divine," he said, "divine!" And Ailsa Brimley, opposite him, smiled gently.

"How are you going to spend your retirement, Mr. Fielding," she asked. "Drinking Frankenwein?"

His glass still held before his lips he looked into the candles. The silver was good, better than his own. He wondered why they were only dining three. "In peace," he replied at last. "I have recently made a discovery."

"What's that?"

"That I have been playing to an empty house. But now I'm comforted to think that no one remembers how I forgot my words or missed an entry. So many of us wait patiently for our audience to die. At Carne no one will remember for more than a Half or two what a mess I've made of life. I was too vain to realise that until recently." He put the glass down in front of him and smiled suddenly at Ailsa Brimley. "That is the peace I mean. Not to exist in anyone's mind, but my own; to be a secular monk, safe and forgotten."

Smiley gave him more wine: "Miss Brimley knew your brother Adrian well in the war. We were all in the same department," he said. "She was Adrian's secretary for a while. Weren't you, Brim?"

"It's depressing how the bad live on," Fielding declared. "Rather embarrassing. For the bad, I mean." He gave a little gastronomic sigh. "The moment of truth in a good meal! *Übergansperiode* between *entremet* and dessert," and they all laughed, and then were silent. Smiley put down his glass, and said:

"The story you told me on Thursday, when I came and saw you . . ."

"Well?" Fielding was irritated.

"About cheating for Tim Perkins . . . how you took the paper from the case and altered it . . ."

"Yes?"

"It isn't true." He might have been talking about the weather. "They've examined it and it isn't true. The writing was all one person's . . . the boy's. If anyone cheated, it must have been the boy."

There was a long silence. Fielding shrugged.

"My dear fellow, you can't expect me to believe that. These people are practically moronic."

"Of course, it doesn't necessarily signify anything. I mean you could be protecting the boy, couldn't you? By lying for him, for his honour so to speak. Is that the explanation?"

"I've told you the truth," he replied shortly. "Make what you want of it."

"I mean, I can see a situation where there might have been collusion, where you were moved by the boy's distress when he brought you the papers; and on the spur of the moment you opened the case and took out his paper and told him what to write."

"Look here," said Fielding hotly, "why don't you keep off this? What's it got to do with you?" And Smiley replied with sudden fervour:

"I'm trying to help, Fielding. I beg you to believe me, I'm trying to help. For Adrian's sake. I don't want there to be . . . more trouble than there need, more pain. I want to get it straight before Rigby comes. They've dropped the charge against Janie. You know that, don't you? They seem to think it's Rode, but they haven't pulled him in. They could have done, but they haven't. They just took more statements from him. So you see, it matters terribly about the writing-case. Everything hangs by whether you really saw inside it; and whether Perkins did. Don't you see that? If it was Perkins who cheated after all, if it was only the boy who opened the case and not you, then they'll want to know the answer to a very important question: *they'll want to know how you knew what was inside it.*"

"What are you trying to say?"

"They're not really moronic, you know. Let's start from the other end for a moment. Suppose it was you who killed Stella Rode, suppose you had a reason, a terribly good reason, and they knew what that reason might be; suppose you went ahead of Rode after giving him the case that night—by bicycle, for instance, like Janie said, riding on the wind. If that were really so, none of those things you saw would have been in the case at all. You could have made it up. And when later

the exam. results came out and you realised that Perkins had cheated, then you guessed he had seen inside
the case, had seen that it contained nothing, *nothing but
exam. papers*. I mean that would explain why you had
to kill the boy." He stopped and glanced towards Fielding. "And in a way," he added almost reluctantly, "it
makes better sense, doesn't it?"

"And what, may I ask, was the reason you speak
of?"

"Perhaps she blackmailed you. She certainly knew
about your conviction in the war from when she was up
North. Her father was a magistrate, wasn't he? I understand they've looked up the files. The police, I mean. It
was her father who heard the case. She knew you were
broke and needed another job and she kept you on a
hook. It seems D'Arcy knew too. She told him. She'd
nothing to lose; he was in on the story from the start,
he'd never allow the papers to get hold of it; she knew
that, she knew her man. Did *you* tell D'Arcy as well,
Fielding? I think you may have done. When she came
to you and told you she knew, jeered and laughed at
you, you went to D'Arcy and told him. You asked him
what to do. And he said—what would he say?—
perhaps he said find out what she wants. But she
wanted nothing; not money at least, but something more
pleasing, more gratifying to her twisted little mind: she
wanted to command and own you. She loved to con-
spire, she summoned you to meetings at absurd times
and places; in woods, in disused churches, and above all
at night. And she wanted nothing from you but your
will, she made you listen to her boasts and her mad in-
trigues, made you fawn and cringe, then let you run
away till the next time." He looked up again. "They
might think along those lines, you see. That's why we
need to know who saw inside the case. And who
cheated in the exam." They were both looking at him,
Ailsa in horror, Fielding motionless, impassive.

"If they think that," asked Fielding at last, "how
do they suppose I knew Rode would come back for the
case that night?"

"Oh, they knew she was expecting you to meet her

that night, after the dinner at your house." Smiley threw this off as if it were a tedious detail, "It was part of the game she liked to play."

"How do they know that?"

"From what Rode says," Smiley continued, "Stella was carrying the case in the hall, actually had it in her hand. When they arrived at North Fields she was without it; she flew into a rage and accused him of forgetting it. She made him go back for it. You see the inference?"

"Oh, clearly," said Fielding, and Smiley heard Ailsa Brimley whisper his name in horror.

"In other words, when Stella devised this trick to gratify her twisted will, you saw it as an opportunity to kill her, putting the blame on a non-existent tramp, or, failing that, on Rode, as a second line of defence. Let us suppose you had been meaning to kill her. You had meant, I expect, to ride out there one night when Rode was teaching late. You had your boots and your cape, even the cable stolen from Rode's room, and you meant to lay a false trail. But what a golden opportunity when Perkins turned up with the hand-case! Stella wanted her meeting—the forgotten hand-case was agreed upon as the means of achieving it. That, I fear, is the way their minds may work. And you see, they *know* it wasn't Rode."

"How do they know? How *can* they know? He's got no alibi." Smiley didn't seem to hear. He was looking towards the window, and the heavy velvet curtains stirring uneasily.

"What's that? What are you looking at?" Fielding asked with sudden urgency, but Smiley did not answer.

"You know, Fielding," he said at last, "we just don't know what people are like, we can never tell; there isn't any truth about human beings, no formula that meets each one of us. And there are some of us— aren't there?—who are nothing, who are so labile that we astound ourselves; we're the chameleons. I read a story once about a poet who bathed himself in cold fountains so that he could recognise his own existence in the contrast. He had to reassure himself, you see, like a child being hateful to its parents. You might say he had to make the sun shine on him so that he could see his shadow and feel alive."

Fielding made an impatient movement with his hand. "How do you know it wasn't Rode?"

"The people who are like that—there really are some, Fielding—do you know their secret? They can't feel anything inside them, no pleasure or pain, no love or hate; they're ashamed and frightened that they can't feel. And their shame, this shame, Fielding, drives them to extravagance and colour; they must make themselves feel that cold water, and without that they're nothing. The world sees them as showmen, fantasists, liars, as sensualists perhaps, not for what they are: the living dead."

"How do you know? How do you know it wasn't Rode?" Fielding cried with anger in his voice, and Smiley replied: "I'll tell you."

"If Rode murdered his wife, he had planned to do so long ago. The plastic cape, the boots, the weapon, the intricate timing, the use of Perkins to carry the case to your house—these are evidence of long premeditation. Of course one could ask: if that's so, why did he bother with Perkins at all—why didn't he keep the case with him all the time? But never mind. Let's see how he does it. He walks home with his wife after dinner, having deliberately forgotten the writing-case. Having left Stella at home, he returns to your house to collect it. It was a risky business, incidentally, leaving that case behind. Quite apart from the fact that one would expect him to have locked it, his wife might have noticed he hadn't got it as they left—or you might have noticed, or Miss Truebody—but luckily no one did. He collects the case, hurries back, kills her, fabricating the clues which mislead the police. He thrusts the cape, boots and gloves into the refugees' parcel, ties it up and prepares to make good his escape. He is alarmed by Mad Janie, perhaps, but reaches the lane and re-enters the house as Stanley Rode. Five minutes later he is with the D'Arcys. From then on for the next forty-eight hours he is under constant supervision. Perhaps you didn't know this, Fielding, but the police found the murder weapon four miles down the road in a ditch. They found it within ten hours of the murder being discovered, long before Rode had a chance to throw it there.

"This is the point, though, Fielding. This is what they can't get over. I suppose it would be possible to make a phony murder weapon. Rode could have taken hairs from Stella's comb, stuck them with human blood to a length of coaxial cable and planted the thing in a ditch *before* he committed the murder. But the only blood he could use was his own—which belongs to a different blood group. The blood on the weapon they found belonged to Stella's blood group. He didn't do it. There's a rather more concrete piece of evidence, to do with the parcel. Rigby had a word with Miss Truebody yesterday. It seems she telephoned Stella Rode on the morning of the day she was murdered. Telephoned at your request, Fielding, to say a boy would be bringing some old clothes up to North Fields on Thursday morning—would she be sure to keep the parcel open till then? . . . What did Stella threaten to do, Fielding? Write an anonymous letter to your next school?"

Then Smiley put his hand on Fielding's arm and said: "Go now, in God's name go now. There's very little time, for Adrian's sake go now," and Ailsa Brimley whispered something he could not hear.

Fielding seemed not to hear. His great head was thrown back, his eyes half closed, his wine glass still held between his thick fingers.

And the front-door bell rang out, like the scream of a woman in an empty house.

Smiley never knew what made the noise, whether it was Fielding's hands on the table as he stood up, or his chair, falling backwards. Perhaps it was not a noise at all, but simply the shock of violent movement when it was least expected; the sight of Fielding, who a moment before had sat lethargic in his chair, springing forward across the room. Then Rigby was holding him, had

taken Fielding's right arm and done something to it so
that Fielding cried out in pain and fear, swinging round
to face them under the compulsion of Rigby's grip.
Then Rigby was saying the words, and Fielding's terrified gaze fell upon Smiley.

"Stop him, stop him, Smiley, for God's sake!
They'll hang me." And he shouted the last two words
again and again: "Hang me, hang me," until the detectives came in from the street, and shoved him without
ceremony into a waiting car.

Smiley watched the car go. It didn't hurry, just
picked its way down the wet street and disappeared. He
remained there long after it had gone, looking towards
the end of the road, so that passers-by stared oddly at
him, or tried to follow his gaze. But there was nothing
to see. Only the half-lit street, and the shadows moving
along it.

ABOUT THE AUTHOR

John le Carré was born in 1931. After attending
the universities of Berne and Oxford, he taught
at Eton and spent five years in the British Foreign
Service. *The Spy Who Came In from the Cold,*
his third book, secured him a worldwide reputation. He divides his time between England and
the Continent.

THE WORLD
OF
JOHN LE CARRÉ

He is the preeminent spy novelist of our time, having achieved this honor following the publication of only his third book. Yet THE SPY WHO CAME IN FROM THE COLD, long considered *the* classic spy story, was barely an indication of the brilliant career that has now spanned three decades. From the cold war and the world of George Smiley and beyond to terrorism and the age of *glasnost*, John le Carré has—by anticipating tomorrow's headlines—continually reinvented the espionage thriller.

■

CALL FOR THE DEAD

George Smiley is bitter, weary—he has seen too much and done too much—yet he cannot refuse one last desperate call for . . . the dead. The baffling case will bring him into contact with a British civil servant, a former hero of the German underground and a once-beautiful woman with a terrifying secret. Smiley's case begins with a death that should never have happened . . .

He felt safe in the taxi. Safe and warm. The warmth was contraband, smuggled from his bed and hoarded against the wet January night. Safe because unreal: it was his ghost that ranged the London streets and took note of their unhappy pleasure-seekers, scuttling under commissionaires' umbrellas; and of the tarts, gift-wrapped in polythene. It was his ghost, he decided, which had climbed from the well of sleep and stopped the telephone shrieking on the bedside table . . . Oxford Street . . . why was London the only capital in the world that lost its personality at night? Smiley, as he pulled his coat more closely about him, could think of nowhere, from Los Angeles to Bern, which so readily gave up its daily struggle for identity.

The cab turned into Cambridge Circus, and Smiley sat up with a jolt. He remembered why the Duty Officer had rung, and the memory woke him brutally from his dreams. The conversation came back to him word for word—a feat of recollection long ago achieved.

"Duty Officer speaking, Smiley. I have the Adviser on the line. . . ."

"Smiley; Maston speaking. You interviewed Samuel Arthur Fennan at the Foreign Office on Monday, am I right?"

"Yes . . . yes I did."

"What was the case?"

"Anonymous letter alleging Party membership at Oxford. Routine interview, authorised by the Director of Security."

(Fennan *can't* have complained, thought Smiley; he knew I'd clear him. There was nothing irregular, nothing.)

"Did you go for him at all? Was it hostile, Smiley, tell me that?"

(Lord, he does sound frightened. Fennan must have put the whole Cabinet on to us.)

"No. It was a particularly friendly interview; we liked one another, I think. As a matter of fact I exceeded my brief in a way."

"How, Smiley, how?"

"Well, I more or less told him not to worry."

"You *what?*"

"I told him not to worry; he was obviously in a bit of a state, and so I told him."

"*What* did you tell him?"

"I said I had no powers and nor had the Service; but I could see no reason why we should bother him further."

"Is that all?"

Smiley paused for a second; he had never known Maston like this, never known him so dependent.

"Yes, that's all. Absolutely all." (He'll never forgive me for this. So much for the studied calm, the cream shirts and silver ties, the smart luncheons with ministers.)

"He says you cast doubts on his loyalty, that his career in the F.O. is ruined, that he is the victim of paid informers."

"He said *what?* He must have gone stark mad. He knows he's cleared. What else does he want?"

"Nothing. He's dead. Killed himself at 10:30 this evening. Left a letter to the Foreign Secretary. The police rang one of his secretaries and got permission to open the letter. Then they told us. There's going to be an enquiry. Smiley, you're sure, aren't you?"

"Sure of what?"

". . . never mind. Get round as soon as you can."

■

A MURDER OF QUALITY

George Smiley has emerged from retirement to solve another baffling case of bloody British crime. A woman as dangerous as she is charming . . . a man haunted by his past . . . the murderer hiding amid the Establishment . . . and a clue that is just too impossible to believe . . .

"**I**f you want me to help, I'd be delighted," said Smiley at last. "But give me the facts first."

"Stella Rode was murdered between about ten past eleven and quarter to twelve on the night of Wednesday the sixteenth. She must have been struck fifteen to twenty times with a cosh or bit of piping or something. It was a terrible murder . . . terrible. There are marks all over her body. At a guess I would say she came from the drawing room to the front door to answer the bell or something, when she opened the door she was struck down and dragged to the conservatory. The conservatory door was unlocked, see?"

"I see. . . . It's odd that he should have known that, isn't it?"

"The murderer may have been hiding there already; we can't tell from the prints just there. He was wearing boots—wellington boots, size 10½. We would guess from the spacing of the footprints in the garden that he was about six foot tall. When he had got her to the conservatory he must have hit her again and again—mainly on the head. There's a lot of what we call travelled blood in the conservatory, that's to say, blood spurted from an open artery. There's no sign of that anywhere else."

"And no sign of it on her husband?"

"I'll come to that later, but the short answer is, no." He paused a moment and continued:

"Now, I said there were footprints, and so there were. The murderer came through the back garden. Where he came from and went to, Heaven alone knows. You see, there are no tracks leading away—not wellingtons. None at all. Of course, it's possible the outgoing tracks followed the path to the front gate and got lost in all the to-ing and fro-ing later that night. But I don't think we'd have lost them even then." He glanced at Smiley, then went on:

"He left one thing behind him in the conservatory—an old cloth belt, navy blue, from a cheap overcoat by the look of it. We're working on that now."

"Was she . . . robbed or anything?"

"No sign of interference. She was wearing a string of green beads round her neck, and they've gone, and it looks as though he tried to get the rings off her finger, but they were too tight." He paused.

"I need hardly tell you that we've had reports from every corner of the country about tall men in blue overcoats and gumboots. But none of them had wings as far as I know. Or seven-league boots for jumping from the conservatory to the road."

THE SPY WHO CAME IN
FROM THE COLD

A perilous and final assignment for an agent desperate to end his espionage career—to "come in from the cold"—sets the stage for the triumphant novel that changed the way the game is played, and secured John le Carré's renown as "the world's greatest fictional spymaster."*

"Tell me," Control continued, "are you tired of spying? Forgive me if I repeat the question. I mean that is a phenomenon we understand here, you know. Like aircraft designers . . . metal fatigue, I think the term is. Do say if you are."

Leamas remembered the flight home that morning and wondered.

"If you were," Control added, "we would have to find some other way of taking care of Mundt. What I have in mind is a little out of the ordinary."

The girl came in with the coffee. She put the tray on the desk and poured out two cups. Control waited till she had left the room.

"Such a *silly* girl," he said, almost to himself. "It seems extraordinary they can't find good ones any more. I do wish Ginnie wouldn't go on holiday at times like this." He stirred his coffee disconsolately for a while.

"We really must discredit Mundt," he said. "Tell me, do you drink a lot? Whisky and that kind of thing?"

Leamas had thought he was used to Control.

"I drink a bit. More than most, I suppose."

Control nodded understandingly. "What do you know about Mundt?"

"He's a killer. He was here a year or two back with the East German Steel Mission. We had an adviser here then: Maston."

"Quite so."

"Mundt was running an agent, the wife of an F.O. man. He killed her."

"He tried to kill George Smiley. And of course he shot the woman's husband. He is a very distasteful man. Ex Hitler-

Youth and all that kind of thing. Not at all the intellectual kind of Communist. A practitioner of the cold war.''

''Like us,'' Leamas observed drily.

Control didn't smile. ''George Smiley knew the case well. He isn't with us any more, but I think you ought to ferret him out. He's doing things on seventeenth-century Germany. He lives in Chelsea, just behind Sloane Square. Bywater Street, do you know it?''

''Yes.''

''And Guillam was on the case as well. He's in Satellites Four, on the first floor. I'm afraid everything's changed since your day.''

''Yes.''

''Spend a day or two with them. They know what I have in mind. Then I wondered if you'd care to stay with me for the weekend. My wife,'' he added hastily, ''is looking after her mother, I'm afraid. It will be just you and I.''

''Thanks. I'd like to.''

''We can talk about things in comfort then. It would be very nice. I think you might make a lot of money out of it. You can have whatever you make.''

''Thanks.''

''That is, of course, if you're *sure you want* to . . . no mental fatigue or anything?''

''If it's a question of killing Mundt, I'm game.''

''Do you really feel that?''

■

THE LOOKING GLASS WAR

Against the skylines of London and Berlin, three men play a double-sided game that calls for a different kind of fighting—they must get their military intelligence any way they can, even if it means treachery, betrayal . . . murder.

Taylor had never seen such a sky. Limitless, it curved downward to the snowbound fields, its destiny broken here and there by films of mist which frosted the clustered stars and drew a line round the yellow half-moon. Taylor was frightened, like a landsman frightened by the sea. He hastened his uncertain step, swaying as he went.

He had been walking about five minutes when the car caught him up. There was no footpath. He became aware of its headlights first, because the sound of its engine was deadened by the snow, and he only noticed a light ahead of him, not realizing where it came from. It traced its way languidly over the snowfields and for a time he thought it was the beacon from the airport. Then he saw his own shadow shortening on the road, the light became suddenly brighter, and he knew it must be a car. He was walking on the right, stepping briskly along the edge of the icy rubble that lined the road. He observed that the light was unusually yellow and he guessed the headlights were masked according to the French rule. He was rather pleased with this little piece of deduction; the old brain was pretty clear after all.

He didn't look over his shoulder because he was a shy man in his way and did not want to give the impression of asking for a lift. But it did occur to him, a little late perhaps, that on the Continent they actually drove on the right, and that therefore strictly speaking he was walking on the wrong side of the road and ought to do something about it.

The car hit him from behind, breaking his spine. For one dreadful moment Taylor described a classic posture of anguish, his head and shoulders flung violently backward, fingers extended. He made no cry. It was as if his entire body and soul were concentrated in this final attitude of pain, more articulate in death than any sound the living man had made.

The car carried him for a yard or two then threw him aside, dead on the empty road, a stiff, wrecked figure at the fringe of the wilderness. His trilby hat lay beside him. A blast seized it, carrying it across the snow. The shreds of his pebble-weave coat fluttered in the wind, reaching vainly for the zinc capsule as it rolled gently with the camber to lodge for a moment against the frozen bank, then to continue wearily down the slope.

■
A SMALL TOWN IN GERMANY

In a small town in Germany there lies a secret on which England's survival, Germany's future, and the fate of the world depends. In London a tough investigator faces his most challenging case, and in Bonn the disappearance of a British diplomat may be murder, or worse—defection.

S tepping back into the fresh air, Bradfield found himself face to face with Meadowes, who had quietly left his place beside his daughter and followed him to the back of the church.

"He's vanished," Meadowes said, dreadfully quietly. "I've checked everywhere. Sick list, the doctor; I've been to his house. His car's in the garage; he's not used his milk. No one's seen or heard of him since Friday. He didn't come to Exiles. It was a special occasion for my daughter's birthday, but he didn't come to that either. He'd got engagements, but he was going to look in. He'd promised her a hair dryer as a present; it's not like him, Mr. Bradfield, it's not his way at all."

For one moment, just for a moment, Bradfield's composure seemed to desert him. He stared furiously at Meadowes, then back at the church, as if undecided which to destroy; as if in either anger or despair he would rush down the path and burst open the doors and cry out the news to those who waited so complacently within.

"Come with me."

Even as they entered the main gates of the Embassy and long before the police check cleared them, they could recognize the signs of crisis. Two army motorcycles were parked on the front lawn. Cork, the coding clerk on call, was waiting on the steps, an Everyman guide to investments still in his hand. A green German police van, its blue light flashing, had stationed itself beside the canteen, and they could hear the crackle of its radio.

"Thank the Lord you've come, sir," said Macmullen, the head guard. "I sent the duty driver down; he must have passed you on the carriageway."

All over the building bells were ringing.

"There's a message in from Hanover, sir, from the consulate general; I didn't hear too well. The rally's gone mad, sir; all 'hell's broken loose. They're storming the library and they're going to march on the Consulate; I don't know what the world's coming to; worse than Grosvenor Square. I could hear their screaming on the telephone, sir.''

Meadowes followed Bradfield hastily up the stairs.

"You said a hair dryer? He was giving your daughter a hair dryer?"

It was a moment of deliberate inconsequence, of deliberate slowness perhaps, a nervous gesture before battle was joined. Meadowes at least construed it thus.

"He'd ordered it specially," he said.

"Never mind," said Bradfield, and was about to enter the coding room when Meadowes addressed him once more.

"The file's gone," he whispered. "The Green file for the special minutes. It's been gone since Friday."

■

THE NAIVE AND SENTIMENTAL LOVER

Le Carré's hero is Aldo Cassidy, a tycoon caught frantically between two astonishing loves: Shamus, a wild artist renowned for his carouses, and Helen, the artist's wife, and an alluring beauty. Here is le Carré's disturbing tale of obsessive love and mystery, a brilliant departure from the author's novels of espionage and hailed by *The Times* (London) as "Splendid, original . . . le Carré shows how endowed he is with the art of storytelling."

He called this process *taking the feel of the place*. It was one he had rehearsed often and which involved the sampling of many intangible elements. The setting for instance: is it hostile or amicable? Does it offer seclusion, which is desirable, or isolation, which is not? Does it embrace the occupant, or expose him? Was he—a vital question—born here, is *that* a feasibility?

Despite the cold, his initial impressions were not unfavourable. The park, which clearly provided the view from the principal windows of the house, had a lush pastoral quality which was distinctly soothing. The trees were deciduous (a rare advantage since he secretly found conifers too bleak) and their great age imbued them with a fatherly gentleness.

He listened.

The wind had dropped and the rooks were slowly settling. From the moor, where the sea fog still clung, the rasp of a handsaw vied with the grumbling of livestock. He examined the grazing. Good fencing there, ample space for ponies provided there was no yew to poison them. He had read somewhere, probably in Cobbett, whose *Rural Rides* he had studied for School Certificate, that yew poisoned ponies, and it was one of those aimless cruelties of nature which had remained impressed upon his memory.

Palominos, that was the word.

I shall have palominos. No need for shelter; the chestnuts will provide the shelter. The Welsh variety is best: hardy beasts he had heard from all sides, self-sufficient and cheap to run. The right temperament too: townsmen could manhandle them without danger of reprisal.

He sniffed the air.

Woodsmoke, damp pine, and the indefinable mustiness that is fostered by neglect. I find no fault with it.

Now at last, quite coolly in his outward manner, he turned to the house and gave it his critical attention. A deep silence had fallen over the hilltop. In the trees nothing stirred. The shirt hung motionless from its cable. For long minutes he remained as if in prayer, his gloved hands loosely linked over his stomach, his shoulders well back, his fair head a little to one side, a survivor mourning his lost comrades.

"Hullo lover," a pleasant voice said. "Looking for someone, are we?"

■

TINKER, TAILOR,
SOLDIER, SPY

The return of George Smiley brought John le Carré to greater heights in TINKER, TAILOR, SOLDIER, SPY, the first in "The Quest for Karla" trilogy. A mole—a Soviet double agent—has burrowed his way into the most sensitive levels of British intelligence. There, at the secret heart of clandestine operations, Smiley must wrestle with the devastating truth he will uncover.

Alone, Smiley stood at the further end of the paddock, under the dripping trees, trying to make sense of his emotions while he reached for breath. Like an old illness, his anger had taken him by surprise. Ever since his retirement, he had been denying its existence, steering clear of anything that could touch it off: newspapers, former colleagues, gossip of the Martindale sort. After a lifetime of living by his wits and his considerable memory, he had given himself full time to the profession of forgetting. He had forced himself to pursue scholarly interests which had served him well enough as a distraction while he was at the Circus, but which now that he was unemployed were nothing, absolutely nothing. He could have shouted: Nothing!

"Burn the lot," Ann had suggested helpfully, referring to his books. "Set fire to the house. But don't rot."

If by rot, she meant conform, she was right to read that as his aim. He had tried, really tried, as he approached what the insurance advertisements were pleased to call the evening of his life, to be all that a model *rentier* should be; though no one, least of all Ann, thanked him for the effort. Each morning as he got out of bed, each evening as he went back to it, usually alone, he had reminded himself that he never was and never had been indispensable. He had schooled himself to admit that in those last wretched months of Control's career, when disasters followed one another with heady speed, he had been guilty of seeing things out of proportion. And if the old professional Adam rebelled in him now and then and said: You *know* the place went bad, you *know* Jim Prideaux was betrayed—and what more eloquent testimony is there than a bullet, two bullets, in the back? Well, he had replied, suppose he did? And suppose he was right? "It is sheer vanity to believe that one fat middle-aged spy is the only person capable of holding the world together," he would tell himself. And other times: "I never heard of anyone yet who left the Circus without some unfinished business."

Only Ann, though she could not read his workings, refused to accept his findings. She was quite passionate, in fact, as only women can be on matters of business, really driving him to go back, take up where he had left off, never to veer aside in favour of the easy arguments. Not of course that she knew anything, but what woman was ever stopped by a want of information? She felt. And despised him for not acting in accordance with her feelings.

And now, at the very moment when he was near enough beginning to believe his own dogma, a feat made no easier by Ann's infatuation for an out-of-work actor, what happens but that the assembled ghosts of his past—Lacon, Control, Karla, Alleline, Esterhase, Bland, and finally Bill Haydon himself—barge into his cell and cheerfully inform him, as they drag him back to this same garden, that everything he had been calling vanity is truth?

"Haydon," he repeated to himself, no longer able to stem the tides of memory. Even the name was like a jolt. "I'm told that you and Bill shared *everything* once upon a time," said Martindale. He stared at his chubby hands, watching them shake. Too old? Impotent? Afraid of the chase? Or afraid of what he might unearth at the end of it? "There are always a dozen reasons for doing nothing," Ann liked to say—it was a favourite apologia, indeed, for many of her misdemeanours. "There is only one reason for doing *something*. And that's because you want to." Or have to? Ann would furiously deny it: coercion, she would say, is just another word for doing what you want; or for not doing what you are afraid of.

THE HONOURABLE SCHOOLBOY

Jerry Westerby is "The Honourable Schoolboy," a seasoned but reckless secret agent. George Smiley is chief of the battered British Soviet Service, seeking revenge against the Soviet double agent who betrayed them. In Hong Kong the game begins, and in London a lifetime obsession escalates, in this, the second novel of the Karla trilogy . . .

Smiley walked, one round little man in a raincoat. Social journalists with more class than Jerry, shrewdly observing his progress through the purlieus of the Charing Cross Road, would have recognised the type at once: the mackintosh brigade personified, cannon-fodder of the mixed-sauna parlours and the naughty bookshops. These long tramps had become a habit for him; with his newfound energy he could cover half the length of London and not notice it. From Cambridge Circus, now that he knew the byways, he could take any of twenty routes and never cross the same path twice. Having selected a beginning, he would let luck and instinct guide him while his other mind plundered the remoter regions of his soul.

But this evening his journey had a pull to it, drawing him south and westward, and Smiley yielded. The air was damp and cold, hung with a harsh fog that had never seen the sun. Walking, he took his own island with him, and it was crammed with images, not people. Like an extra mantle, the white walls encased him in his thoughts. In a doorway, two murderers in leather coats were whispering; under a streetlamp, a dark-haired boy angrily clutched a violin case. Outside a theatre, a waiting crowd burned in the blaze of lights from the awning overhead, and the fog curled round them like fire smoke.

Never had Smiley gone into battle knowing so little and expecting so much. He felt lured, and he felt pursued. Yet when he tired, and drew back for a moment, and considered the logic of what he was about, it almost eluded him. He glanced back and saw the jaws of failure waiting for him. He peered forward and through his moist spectacles saw the phantoms of great hopes dancing in the mist. He blinked around him and knew there was nothing for him where he stood. Yet he advanced without the ultimate conviction.

It was no answer to rehearse the steps that had brought him to his point—the Russian gold seam, the imprint of Karla's private army, the thoroughness of Haydon's efforts to extinguish knowledge of them. Beyond the limits of these external reasons, Smiley perceived in himself the existence of a darker motive, infinitely more obscure, one which his rational mind continued to reject. He called it Karla, and it was true that somewhere in him, like a leftover legend, there burned the embers of hatred toward the man who had set out to destroy the temples of his private faith, whatever remained of them: the service that he loved, his friends, his country, his concept of a reasonable balance in human affairs. It was true also that a lifetime or two ago, in a sweltering Indian jail, the two men had actually faced each other, Smiley and Karla, across an iron table, though Smiley had no reason at the time to know he was in the presence of his destiny. Karla's head was on the block in Moscow; Smiley had tried to woo him to the West, and Karla had kept silent, preferring death or worse to an easy defection. And it was true that now and then the memory of that encounter, of Karla's unshaven face and watchful, inward eyes, came at him like a spectre out of the murk of his little room while he slept fitfully on his bunk.

But hatred was really not an emotion he could sustain for any length of time, unless it was the obverse side of love.

∎

SMILEY'S PEOPLE

In SMILEY'S PEOPLE, le Carré gives us the last chapter . . . the final agonizing confrontation between George Smiley and Karla, his mortal enemy and opposite number inside the Soviet Union. A British agent has been murdered, and once again Smiley is called in . . .

"George! You look worried. Don't be. We're all in the clear on this. All of us!"

"I'm not worried, Oliver."

"You look as though you're reproaching yourself. I can tell!"

"When agents die—" said Smiley, but left the sentence incomplete, and anyway Lacon couldn't wait for him. He strode off again, a hiker with miles to go. Lacon, Strickland, Mostyn, thought Smiley as Strickland's Aberdonian brogue hammered on. One Cabinet Office factotum, one Circus fixer, one scared boy. Why not real people? Why not Vladimir's case officer, whoever he is? Why not Saul Enderby, their Chief?

A verse of Auden's rang in his mind from the days when he was Mostyn's age: *Let us honour if we can/The vertical man/Though we value none/But the horizontal one.* Or something.

And why Smiley? he thought. Above all, why me? Of all people, when as far as they're concerned I'm deader than old Vladimir.

"Will you have tea, Mr. Smiley, or something stronger?" called Mostyn through the open kitchen doorway. Smiley wondered whether he was naturally so pale.

"He'll have tea only, thank you, Mostyn!" Lacon blurted, making a sharp about-turn. "After shock, tea is a deal safer. With sugar, right, George? Sugar replaces lost energy. Was it *gruesome,* George! How perfectly awful for you."

No, it wasn't awful, it was the truth, thought Smiley. He was shot and I saw him dead. Perhaps you should do that too.

Apparently unable to leave Smiley alone, Lacon had come back down the room and was peering at him with clever, uncomprehending eyes. He was a mawkish creature, sudden but without spring, with youthful features cruelly aged and a raw unhealthy rash around his neck where his shirt had scuffed the skin. In the religious light between dawn and morning his black waistcoat and white collar had the glint of the soutane.

"I've hardly said hullo," Lacon complained, as if it were Smiley's fault. "George. Old friend. My goodness."

"Hullo, Oliver," said Smiley.

Still Lacon remained there, gazing down at him, his long head to one side, like a child studying an insect. In his memory Smiley replayed Lacon's fervid phone call of two hours before.

It's an emergency, George. You remember Vladimir? George, are you awake? You remember the old General, George? Used to live in Paris?

Yes, I remember the General, he had replied. Yes, Oliver, I remember Vladimir.

We need someone from his past, George. Someone who knew his little ways, can identify him, damp down potential scandal. We need you, George. Now.

THE LITTLE DRUMMER GIRL

A terrifying adventure of a young actress forced to play the ultimate role . . . that of a dangerous and elusive terrorist leader. Here le Carré explores new labyrinths of intrigue, journeys into the dark heart of modern-day terrorism and, in this "theatre of the real," builds to a final, frightening deception . . .

"So, Charlie, what we propose," said Kurtz in a slower, more genial voice, "we propose an open-ended audition, a string of questions which we invite you to answer very frankly, very truthfully, even though for the meanwhile remaining necessarily in the dark about the purpose of them."

He paused but she didn't speak, and there was by now a tacit submission in her silence.

"We ask you never to evaluate, never to try to come to our side of the net, never to seek to please or gratify us in any regard. Many things you might consider negative in your life we would surely see differently. Do not attempt to do our thinking for us." A short jab of the forearm entrenched this amicable warning. "Question. What happens—whether now or later—what happens should either one of us elect to jump off the escalator? Charlie, let me try to answer that."

"You do that, Mart," she advised, and, putting her elbows on the table, rested her chin in her hands and smiled at him with a look intended to convey dazed unbelief.

"Thank you, Charlie, so listen carefully, please. Depending on the precise moment you want out or we do, depending on the degree of your knowledge at that time and our assessment of you, we follow one of two courses. Course one, we extract a solemn promise from you, we give you money, we send you back to England. A handshake, mutual trust, good friends, and a certain vigilance on our side to make sure you keep the bargain. You follow me?"

She lowered her gaze to the table, partly to escape his scrutiny, partly to conceal her growing excitement. For that was another thing Kurtz counted on, which most intelligence professionals forget too soon: to the uninitiated, the secret world is of itself attractive. Simply by turning on its axis, it can draw the weakly anchored to its centre.

"Course two, a little rougher, still not terrible. We place you in quarantine. We like you, but we fear we have reached a point where you might compromise our project, where the part we are proposing, say, cannot safely be offered anyplace else while you are at large to talk about it."

She knew without looking that he was smiling his good-hearted smile, suggesting that such frailty on Charlie's part would be only human.

"So what we can do in *that* case, Charlie," he resumed, "we take a nice house somewhere—say, on a beach, somewhere pleasant, no problem. We give you company, some people similar to the kids here. Nice people but able. We fake some reason for your absence, most likely a voguish one that fits your volatile reputation, such as a mystical sojourn to the East."

His thick fingers had found his old wristwatch on the table before him. Without looking at it, Kurtz lifted it and set it down six inches nearer to him. Needing an activity herself, Charlie took up a pen and began to doodle on the pad before her.

"Once you are out of quarantine, we do not desert you—far from it. We straighten you out, we give you a sack of money, we keep in touch with you, make sure you are not incautious in any way, and as soon as it's safe we help you to resume your career and friendships. That's the worst that can happen, Charlie, and I'm only telling it to you because you may be harbouring some crazy notion that by saying 'no' to us, now or later, you're going to wake up dead in a river wearing a pair of concrete boots. We don't deal that way. Least of all with friends."

■

A PERFECT SPY

In le Carré's brilliant masterwork he explores the very essence of espionage and the devastating effect of a missing spy. Magnus Pym is the "perfect spy" and his sudden disappearance triggers fear in the hearts of family, friends, and spy networks on both sides of the Iron Curtain. A desperate international manhunt, A PERFECT SPY is also the absorbing portrait of a complex and tortured life . . .

Pym closed the curtains and put the lights back on. I will make my own daytime and my own night. The briefcase stood where he had left it, strangely rigid from its steel lining. Everybody carried cases, he remembered, as he stared at it. Rick's was pigskin. Lippsie's was cardboard. Poppy's was a scruffy grey thing with marks printed on it to look like hide. And Jack—dear Jack—you have your marvellous old attaché case, faithful as the dog you had to shoot.

Some people, you see, Tom, they leave their bodies to a teaching hospital. The hands go to this class, the heart to that one, the eyes to another, everyone gets something, everyone is grateful. Your father, however, has only his secrets. They're his provenance and his curse.

With a bump, he sat down at the desk.

To tell it straight, he rehearsed. Word for word the truth. No evasions, no fictions, no devices. Just my overpromised self set free.

To tell it to no one in particular, and to everyone. To tell it to all of you who own me, to whom I have given myself with such unthinking liberality. To my handlers and paymasters. To Mary and all the other Marys. To anyone who had a piece of me, was promised more and duly disappointed. And to whatever of myself remained after the great Pym share-out.

To all my creditors and co-owners incorporated, here once and for all the settlement of arrears that Rick so often dreamed of and that shall now be achieved in his only acknowledged son. Whoever Pym was to you, whoever you are or were, here is the last of many versions of the Pym you thought you knew.

* * *

Pym took a deep breath and puffed it out again.

You do it once. Once in your life and that's it. No rewrites, no polishing, no evasions. No would-it-be-better-this-ways. You're the male bee. You do it once, and die.

He took up a pen, then a single sheet of paper. He scribbled some lines, whatever came into his head. All work and no play makes Jack a dull spy. Poppy, Poppy, on the wall. Miss Dubber must a-cruising go. Eat good bread, poor Rickie's dead. Rickie-Tickie father. His hand ran smoothly, not a crossing-out. Sometimes, Tom, we have to do a thing in order to find out the reason for it. Sometimes our actions are questions, not answers.

In John le Carre's latest novel, it is the third uncertain summer of *perestroika* and *glasnost*, and at a small British trade fair in Moscow, a document changes hands that can alter the course of history—if it is delivered to the right person. In this tale of love, betrayal, and courage, John le Carré reinvents the novel of espionage for the post-Cold War era, and shows yet again why he is "the finest spy novelist of this century."*

■

THE RUSSIA HOUSE

by
John le Carre

In a broad Moscow street not two hundred yards from the Leningrad station, on the upper floor of an ornate and hideous hotel built by Stalin in the style known to Muscovites as Empire During the Plague, the British Council's first ever audio fair for the teaching of the English language and the spread of British culture was grinding to its excruciating end. The time was half past five, the summer weather erratic. After fierce rain showers all day long, a false sunlight was blazing in the puddles and raising vapour from the pavements. Of the passers-by, the younger ones wore jeans and sneakers, but their elders were still huddled in their warms.

The room the Council had rented was not expensive but neither was it appropriate to the occasion. —I have seen it. Not long ago, in Moscow on quite another mission, I tiptoed up the great empty staircase and, with a diplomatic passport in my pocket, stood in the eternal dusk that shrouds old ballrooms when they are asleep.—With its plump brown pillars and gilded mirrors, it was better suited to the last hours of a sinking liner than the launch of a great initiative. On the ceiling, snarling Russians in proletarian caps shook their fists at Lenin. Their vigour contrasted unhelpfully with the chipped green racks of sound cassettes along the walls, featuring *Winnie-the-Pooh* and *Advanced Computer English in Three Hours*. The sackcloth sound-booths, locally procured and lacking many of their promised features, had the sadness of deck chairs on a rainy beach. The exhibitors' stands, crammed under the shadow of an over-hanging gallery, seemed as blasphemous as betting shops in a tabernacle.

Nevertheless a fair of sorts had taken place. People had come, as Moscow people do, provided they have the documents and status to satisfy the hard-eyed boys in leather jackets at the door. Out of politeness. Out of curiosity. To talk to Westerners. Because it is there. And now on the fifth and final evening the great farewell cocktail party of exhibitors and invited guests was getting into its stride. A handful of small *nomenklatura* of the Soviet cultural bureaucracy was gathering under the chandelier, the ladies in their beehive hairstyles and flowered frocks designed for slenderer frames, the gentlemen slimmed by the shiny French-tailored suits that signified access to the special clothing stores. Only their British hosts, in despondent shades of grey, observed the monotone of Socialist austerity. The hubbub rose, a brigade of pinafored governesses distributed the curling salami sandwiches and warm white wine. A senior British diplomat who was not quite the Ambassador shook the better hands and said he was delighted.

Only Niki Landau among them had withheld himself from the celebrations. He was stooped over the table in his empty stand, totting up his last orders and checking his dockets against expenses, for it was a maxim of Landau's never to go out and play until he had wrapped up his day's business.

And in the corner of his eye—an anxious blue blur was all that she amounted to—this Soviet woman he was deliberately ignoring. *Trouble,* he was thinking as he laboured. *Avoid.*

The air of festivity had not communicated itself to Landau, festive by temperament though he was. For one thing, he had a lifelong aversion to British officialdom, ever since his father had been forcibly returned to Poland. The British themselves, he told me later, he would hear no wrong of them. He was one of them by adoption and he had the poker-backed reverence of the convert. But the Foreign Office flunkies were another matter. And the loftier they were, and the more they twitched and smirked and raised their stupid eyebrows at him, the more he hated them and thought about his dad. For another thing, if he had been left to himself, he would never have come to the audio fair in the first place. He'd have been tucked up in Brighton with a nice new little friend he had, called Lydia, in a nice little private hotel he knew for taking little friends.

"Better to keep our powder dry till the Moscow book fair in September," Landau had advised his clients at their headquarters on the Western by-pass. "The Russkies love a book, you see, Bernard, but the audio market scares them and they aren't geared for it. Go in with the book fair, we'll clean up. Go in with the audio fair, we're dead."

But Landau's clients were young and rich and did not believe in death. "Niki boy," said Bernard, walking round behind him and putting a hand on his shoulder, which Landau didn't like, "in the world today, we've got to show the flag. We're patriots, see, Niki? Like you. That's why we're an offshore company. With the *glasnost* today, the Soviet Union, it's the Mount Everest of the recording business. And you're going to put us on the top, Niki. Because if you're not, we'll find somebody who will. Somebody younger, Niki, right? Somebody with the drive and the class."

The drive Landau had still. But the class, as he himself was the first to tell you, the class, forget it. He was a card, that's what he liked to be. A pushy, short-arsed Polish card and proud of it. He was Old Nik the cheeky chappie of the Eastward-facing reps, capable, he liked to boast, of selling filthy pictures to a Georgian convent or hair tonic to a Roumanian billiard ball. He was Landau the undersized bedroom athlete, who wore raised heels to give his Slav body the English scale he admired, and ritzy suits that whistled "here I am." When Old Nik set up his stand, his travelling colleagues assured our unattributable enquirers, you could hear the tinkle of the hand-bell on his Polish vendor's barrow.

And little Landau shared the joke with them, he played their game. "Boys, I'm the Pole you wouldn't touch with a barge," he would declare proudly as he ordered up another round. Which was his way of getting them to laugh with him. Instead of at him. And then most likely, to demonstrate his point, he would whip a comb from his top pocket and drop into a crouch. And with the aid of a picture on the wall, or any other polished surface, he'd sweep back his too black hair in preparation for fresh conquest, using both his little hands to coax it into manliness. "Who's that comely one I'm looking at over there in the corner then?" he'd ask, in his godless blend of ghetto Polish and East End cockney. "Hullo there, sweetheart! Why are we suffering all alone tonight?" And once out of five times he'd score, which in Landau's book was an acceptable rate of return, always provided you kept asking.

But this evening Landau wasn't thinking of scoring or even asking. He was thinking that yet again he had worked his heart out all week for a pittance—or, as he put it more graphically to me, a tart's kiss. And that every fair these days, whether it was a book fair or an audio fair or any other kind of fair, took a little more out of him than he liked to admit to himself, just as every woman did. And gave him a fraction too little in return. And that tomorrow's plane back to London couldn't come too soon. And that if this Russian bird didn't stop insinuating herself into his attention when he was trying to close his books and put on his party smile and join the jubilant throng, he would very likely say something to her in her own language that both of them would live to regret.

That she was Russian went without saying. Only a Russian woman would have a plastic perhaps-bag dangling from her arm in readiness for the chance purchase that is the triumph of everyday life, even if most perhaps-bags were of string. Only a Russian would be so nosy as to stand close enough to check a man's arithmetic. And only a Russian would preface her interruption with one of those fastidious grunts, which in a man always reminded Landau of his father doing up his shoe laces, and in a woman, Harry, bed.

"Excuse me, sir. Are you the gentleman from Abercrombie & Blair?" she asked.

"Not here, dear," said Landau without lifting his head. She had spoken English, so he had spoken English in return, which was the way he played it always.

"Mr. Barley?"

"Not Barley, dear. Landau."

"But this is Mr. Barley's stand."

"This is not Barley's stand. This is my stand. Abercrombie & Blair are next door."

Still without looking up, Landau jabbed his pencil-end to the left, towards the empty stand on the other side of the partition, where a green-and-gold board proclaimed the ancient publishing house of Abercrombie & Blair of Norfolk Street, Strand.

"But that stand is empty. No one is there," the woman objected. "It was empty yesterday also."

"Correct. Right on," Landau retorted in a tone that was final enough for everybody. And he ostentatiously lowered himself further into his account book, waiting for the blue blur to remove itself. Which was rude of him, he knew, and her continuing presence made him feel ruder.

"But where is Scott Blair? Where is the man they call Barley? I must speak to him. It is very urgent."

Landau was by now hating the woman with unreasoning ferocity.

"*Mr.* Scott Blair," he began as he snapped up his head and stared at her full on, "more commonly known to his intimates as Barley, is *awol,* madam. That means absent without leave. His company booked a stand—yes. And Mr. Scott Blair is chairman, president, governor-general and for all I know lifetime dictator of that company. However, he did not occupy his stand—" But here, having caught her eye, he began to lose his footing. "Listen, dear, I happen to be trying to make a living here, right? I am not making it for Mr. Barley Scott Blair, love him as I may."

Then he stopped, as a chivalrous concern replaced his momentary anger. The woman was trembling. Not only with the hands that held her brown perhaps-bag but also at the neck, for her prim blue dress was finished with a collar of old lace and Landau could see how it shook against her skin and how her skin was actually whiter than the lace. Yet her mouth and jaw were set with determination and her expression commanded him.

"Please, sir, you must be very kind and help me," she said as if there were no choice.

Now Landau prided himself on knowing women. It was another of his irksome boasts but it was not without foundation. "Women, they're my hobby, my life's study and my consuming passion, Harry," he confided to me, and the conviction in his voice was as solemn as a Mason's pledge. He could no longer tell you how many he had had, but he was pleased to say that the figure ran into the hundreds and there was not one of them who had cause to regret the experience. "I play straight, I choose wisely, Harry," he assured me, tapping one side of his nose with his forefinger. "No cut wrists, no broken marriages, no harsh words afterwards." How true this was nobody would ever know, myself included, but there can be no doubt that the instincts that had guided him through his philanderings came rushing to his assistance as he formed his judgments about the woman.

She was earnest. She was intelligent. She was determined. She was scared, even though her dark eyes were lit with humour. And she had that rare quality which Landau in his flowery way liked to call the Class That Only Nature Can Bestow. In other words, she had quality as well as strength. And since in moments of crisis our thoughts do not run consecutively but rather sweep over us in waves of intuition and experience, he sensed all these things at once and was on terms with them by the time she spoke to him again.

"A Soviet friend of mine has written a creative and important work of literature," she said after taking a deep breath. "It is a novel. A great novel. Its message is important for all mankind."

She had dried up.

"A novel," Landau prompted. And then, for no reason he could afterwards think of, "What's its title, dear?"

The strength in her, he decided, came neither from bravado nor insanity but from conviction.

"What's its message then, if it hasn't got a title?"

"It concerns actions before words. It rejects the gradualism of the *perestroika*. It demands action and rejects all cosmetic change."

"Nice," said Landau, impressed.

She spoke like my mother used to, Harry: chin up and straight into your face.

"In spite of *glasnost* and the supposed liberalism of the new guidelines, my friend's novel cannot yet be published in the Soviet Union," she continued. "Mr. Scott Blair has undertaken to publish it with discretion."

"Lady," said Landau kindly, his face now close to hers. "If your friend's novel is published by the great house of Abercrombie & Blair, believe me, you can be assured of total secrecy."

He said this partly as a joke he couldn't resist and partly because his instincts told him to take the stiffness out of their conversation and make it less conspicuous to anybody watching. And whether she understood the joke or not, the woman smiled also, a swift warm smile of self-encouragement that was like a victory over her fears.

"Then, Mr. Landau, if you love peace please take this manuscript with you back to England and give it immediately to Mr. Scott Blair. Only to Mr. Scott Blair. It is a gift of trust."

What happened next happened quickly, a street-corner trans-action, willing seller to willing buyer. The first thing Landau did was look behind her, past her shoulder. He did that for his own preservation as well as hers. It was his experience that when the Russkies wanted to get up to a piece of mischief, they always had other people close by. But his end of the assembly room was empty, the area beneath the gallery where the stands were was dark and the party at the centre of the room was by now in full cry. The three boys in leather jackets at the front door were talking stodgily among themselves.

His survey completed, he read the girl's plastic name badge on her lapel. which was something he would normally have done earlier but her black-brown eyes had distracted him. Yekaterina Orlova, he read. And underneath, the word "Octo-ber," given in both English and Russian, this being the name of one of Moscow's smaller State publishing houses specialising in translations of Soviet books for export, mainly to other Socialist countries, which I am afraid condemned it to a certain dowdiness.

Next he told her what to do, or perhaps he was already telling her by the time he read her badge. Landau was a street kid, up to all the tricks. The woman might be as brave as six lions and by the look of her probably was. But she was no conspirator. Therefore he took her unhesitatingly into his protection. And in doing so he spoke to her as he would to any woman who needed his basic counsel, such as where to find his hotel bedroom or what to tell her hubby when she got home.

"Got it with you then, have you, dear?" he asked, peering down at the perhaps-bag and smiling like a friend.

"Yes."

"In there, is it?"

"Yes."

"Then give me the whole bag normally," Landau said, talking her through her act. "That's the way. Now give me a friendly Russian kiss. The formal sort. Nice. You've brought me an official farewell gift on the last evening of the fair, you see. Something that will cement Anglo-Soviet relations and make me overweight on the flight home unless I dump it in the dustbin at the airport. Very normal transaction. I must have received half a dozen such gifts today already."

Part of this was spoken while he crouched with his back to her. For, reaching into the bag, he had already slipped out the brown-paper parcel that was inside it and was dropping it deftly into his briefcase, which was of the home filing variety, very compendious, with compartments that opened in a fan.

"Married, are we, Katya?"

No answer. Maybe she hadn't heard. Or she was too busy watching him.

"Is it your husband who's written the novel, then?" said Landau, undeterred by her silence.

"It is dangerous for you," she whispered. "You must believe in what you are doing. Then everything is clear."

As if he had not heard this warning at all, Landau selected, from a pile of samples that he had kept to give away tonight, a four-pack of the Royal Shakespeare Company's specially commissioned reading of *A Midsummer Night's Dream,* which he placed ostentatiously on the table and signed for her on the plastic casing with a felt-tip pen: "From Niki to Katya, Peace," and the date. Then he put the four-pack ceremoniously into the perhaps-bag for her, and gathered the handles of the bag together and pressed them into her hand, because she was becoming lifeless and he was worried she might break down or cease to function. Only then did he give her the reassurance that she seemed to be asking for, while he continued to hold her hand, which was cold, he told me, but nice.

"All of us have got to do something risky now and then, haven't we, dear?" Landau said lightly. "Going to adorn the party, are we?"

"No."

"Like a nice dinner out somewhere?"

"It is not convenient."

"You want me to take you to the door?"

"It doesn't matter."

"I think we've got to smile, dear," he said, still in English as he walked her across the room, chatting to her like the good salesman he had once again become.

Reaching the great landing, he shook her hand. "See you at the book fair, then? September. And thanks for warning me, okay? I'll bear it in mind. Still, the main thing is, we've got a deal. Which is always nice. Right?"

She took his hand and seemed to draw courage from it, for she smiled again and her smile was dazed but grateful, and almost irresistibly warm.

"My friend has made a great gesture," she explained as she pushed back an unruly lock of hair. "Please be sure that Mr. Barley is aware of this."

"I'll tell him. Don't you worry," said Landau jauntily.

He would have liked another smile just for himself, but she had lost interest in him. She was delving in her bag for her card, which he knew she had forgotten till this moment. "ORLOVA, Yekaterina Borisovna," it read, in Cyrillic one side and Roman the other, again with the name "October" in both renderings. She gave it to him, then walked stiffly down the pompous staircase, head up and one hand on the broad marble balustrade, the other hand trailing the perhaps-bag. The boys in leather jackets watched her all the way down to the hall. And Landau, while he popped the card into his top pocket with the half-dozen others he'd collected in the last two hours, saw them watch her and gave the boys a wink. And the boys after due reflection winked back at him, because this was the new season of openness when a pair of good Russian hips could be acknowledged for what they were, even to a foreigner.

For the fifty minutes of revelry that remained, Niki Landau threw his heart into the party. Sang and danced for a grimfaced Scottish librarian in pearls. Recited a witty political anecdote about Mrs. Thatcher for a pair of pale listeners from the State Copyright Agency, VAAP, till they suddenly emitted wild laughter. Buttered up three ladies from Progress Publishers and, in a series of nimble journeys to his briefcase, presented each with a memento of his stay, for Landau was a natural giver and remembered names and promises, just as he remembered so many other things, with the directness of an unencumbered mind. But all the while he kept the briefcase unobtrusively in view, and even before the guests had left, he was holding it in his spare hand while he made his farewells. And when he boarded the private bus that was waiting to take the reps back to their hotel, he sat with it on his knees while he joined in a tuneful unison of rugby songs, led as usual by Spikey Morgan.

"Ladies present now, boys," Landau warned and, standing up, commanded silence at the passages that he considered too broad. But even when he was playing the great conductor he contrived to keep a firm grip on the briefcase.

At the hotel entrance the usual gaggle of pimps, drug-pushers and currency dealers hung around and, together with their KGB minders, watched the group enter. But Landau saw nothing in their behaviour to concern him, whether over-watchful or over-casual. The crippled old warrior who guarded the passageway to the lifts demanded as usual to see his hotel pass, but when Landau, who had already presented him with a hundred Marlboros, asked him accusingly in Russian why he wasn't out flirting with his girlfriend tonight, he gave a rasping laugh and punched him on the shoulder in goodfellowship.

"If they're trying to frame me, I thought, they'd better be quick about it or the trail will be cold, Harry," he told me, taking the part of the opposition rather than his own. "When you frame, Harry, you've got to move in fast while the evidence is still planted on the victim," he explained, as if he had been framing people all his life.

"Bar of the National, nine o'clock then," Spikey Morgan said to him wearily when they had fought their way out at the fourth floor.

"Could be, could be not, Spikey," Landau replied. "I'm not quite myself, to be honest."

"Thank God for that," said Spikey through a yawn, and plodded off into his own dark corridor watched by the evil-eyed floor concierge in her horsebox.

Reaching his bedroom door Landau braced himself before putting the key into the lock. They'd do it now, he thought. Here and now would be the best time to snatch me and the manuscript.

But when he stepped inside, the room was empty and undisturbed and he felt foolish for having suspected it of being any different. Still alive, he thought, and set the briefcase on the bed.

Then he pulled the handkerchief-sized curtains as close as they would go, which was halfway, and hung the useless "Do Not Disturb" notice on the door, which he then locked. He emptied the pockets of his suit, including the pocket where he stored incoming business cards, pulled off his jacket and tie, his metal armbands, finally his shirt. From the fridge he poured himself half an inch of lemon vodka and took a sip. Landau was not a drinker really, he explained to me, but when in Moscow he did like a nice lemon vodka to end his day. Taking his glass to the bathroom, he stood before the mirror and for a good ten minutes anxiously examined the roots of his hair for signs of white, touching out offending spots with the aid of a new formula that was working wonders. Having completed this labour to his satisfaction, he bound his skull with an elaborate rubber turban like a bathing cap and showered, while he sang "I am the very model of a modern major-general" rather well. Then he towelled himself, vigorously for the sake of his muscle-tone, slipped into a bold flowered bathrobe and marched back to the bedroom still singing.

And he did these things partly because he always did them

and needed the steadying familiarity of his own routines, but partly also because he was proud of having thrown caution to the winds for once and not found twenty-five sound reasons for doing nothing, which these days he might have done.

She was a lady, she was afraid, she needed help, Harry. When did Niki Landau ever refuse a lady? And if he was wrong about her, well then she'd made a crying fool of him and he might as well pack up his toothbrush and report himself at the front door of the Lubyanka for five years' study of their excellent graffiti without the option. Because he'd rather be made a fool of twenty times over than turn away that woman without a reason. And so saying, if only in his mind, for he was always alert to the possibility of microphones, Landau drew her parcel from the briefcase and with a certain shyness set to work untying the string but not cutting it, just the way he had been taught by his sainted mother, whose photograph at this moment nestled faithfully in his wallet. They've got the same glow, he thought in pleasant recognition as he worried patiently at the knot. It's the Slav skin. It's the Slav eyes, the smile. Two nice Slav girls together. The only difference was that Katya hadn't finished up in Treblinka.

The knot finally yielded. Landau coiled up the string and laid it on the bed. I have to know, you see, dear, he explained to the woman Yekaterina Borisovna in his mind. I don't want to pry. I'm not the nosy one, but if I've got to con my way through Moscow customs, I'd better know what I'm conning them out of, because it helps.

Delicately so as not to tear it, using both hands, Landau parted the brown paper. He did not see himself as any sort of a hero, or not yet. What was a danger to a Moscow beauty might not be a danger to him. He had grown up hard, it was true. The East End of London had been no rest cure for a ten-year-old Polish immigrant, and Landau had taken his share of split lips, broken noses, smashed knuckles and hunger. But if you had asked him now or at any time in the last thirty years what his definition of a hero was, he would have replied without a second's thought that a hero was the first man out of the back door when they started yelling for volunteers.

One thing he did know as he stared at the contents of that brown-paper parcel: he had the buzz on him. Why he had it was something he could sort out later when there weren't better things to do. But if dodgy work needed to be done tonight, Niki Landau was your man. Because when Niki has the buzz, Harry, no one buzzes better, as the girls all know.

The first thing he saw was the envelope. He registered the three notebooks underneath it and saw that the envelope and notebooks were joined with a thick elastic band, the kind he always saved but never found a use for. But it was the envelope that held him because it had her writing on it—a strict copybook kind of writing that confirmed his pure image of her. One square brown envelope, glued rather messily and addressed "Personal for Mr. Bartholomew Scott Blair, urgent."

Slipping it free of the elastic band, Landau held it to the light but it was opaque and revealed no shadow. He explored it with his finger and thumb. One sheet of thin paper inside, two at most. *Mr. Scott Blair has undertaken to publish it with discretion,* he remembered. *Mr. Landau, if you love peace . . . give it immediately to Mr. Scott Blair. Only to Mr. Scott Blair . . . it is a gift of trust.*

She trusts me too, he thought. He turned the envelope over. The back was blank.

And there being only so much that one may learn from a sealed brown envelope, and since Landau drew the line at reading Barley's or anybody else's personal mail, he opened his briefcase again and, having searched the stationery compartment, extracted from it a plain manila envelope of his own, with the words "From the desk of Mr. Nicholas P. Landau" inscribed tastefully on the flap. Then he popped the brown envelope inside the manila one and sealed it. Then he scribbled the name "Barley" on it and filed it in the compartment marked "Social," which contained such oddities as visiting cards that had been pressed on him by strangers and notes of odd commissions he had undertaken to perform for people—such as the publishing lady who needed refills for her Parker pen or the Ministry of Culture official who wanted a Snoopy T-shirt for his nephew or the lady from October who simply happened to be passing while he was wrapping up his stand.

And Landau did this because with the tradecraft that was instinctive in him, if totally untaught, he knew that his first job was to keep the envelope as far away as possible from the notebooks. If the notebooks were trouble, then he wanted nothing that would link them with the letter. And vice versa. And in this he was entirely right. Our most versatile and erudite trainers, dyed in all the oceans of our Service folklore, would not have told it to him one whit differently.

Only then did he take up the three notebooks and slip off the elastic band he kept one ear cocked for footfalls in the corridor. Three grubby Russian notebooks, he reflected, selecting the top one and turning it slowly over. Bound in crudely illustrated board, the spine in fraying cloth. Two hundred and twenty-four pages of poor-quality, feint-ruled quarto, if Landau remembered correctly from the days when he peddled stationery, Soviet price around twenty kopeks retail from any good stationer, always provided that the delivery had arrived and that you were standing in the right queue on the right day.

Finally he opened the notebook and stared at the first page.

*Vanity Fair